The Pony Rider Boys with the Texas Rangers

or

On the Trail of the Border Bandits

Frank Gee Patchin

1st WORLD
LIBRARY
Literary Society

The Pony Rider Boys with the Texas Rangers

Frank Gee Patchin

© 1st World Library – Literary Society, 2005
PO Box 2211
Fairfield, IA 52556
www.1stworldlibrary.org
First Edition

LCCN: 2004195617

Softcover ISBN: 1-4218-0438-7
Hardcover ISBN: 1-4218-0338-0
eBook ISBN: 1-4218-0538-3

Purchase *"The Pony Rider Boys with the Texas Rangers"*
as a traditional bound book at:
www.1stWorldLibrary.org/purchase.asp?ISBN=1-4218-0438-7

1st World Library Literary Society is a nonprofit
organization dedicated to promoting literacy by:

- Creating a free internet library accessible from any
computer worldwide.
- Hosting writing competitions and offering book
publishing scholarships.

Readers interested in supporting literacy
through sponsorship, donations or
membership please contact:
literacy@1stworldlibrary.org
Check us out at: www.1stworldlibrary.ORG
and start downloading free ebooks today.

CONTENTS

CHAPTER I

EXCITEMENT ON THE WEST FORK

Leaving the main branch of Delaware Creek, a broad, sluggish stream that slowly made its way toward the muddy Pecos River, a party of horsemen turned up the west branch.

Horses and men alike were wearied, dusty, perspiring and sleepy under the glare of a midsummer Texas sun. Little had been said for some time. None felt like talking. For hours they had been working south by west, urged on by the green of the foliage that they could see a short distance ahead. At least it had seemed a short distance for the last five hours, but the green trees now appeared to be just as far away as when the party had first sighted them early in the morning.

At the head of the line rode a grizzled, stern-faced man, sitting on his pony very stiff and erect. Just behind him was a young man, slender, fair haired and smiling, despite the discomfort his red face showed him to be suffering. Still back of them rode three other young men, the last in the line being a disconsolate fat figure of a boy who slouched from side to side in his saddle, each lurch threatening to precipitate him to the ground. The boy's pony was dragging along with nose close to the earth, the bridle rein slipping lower and lower over the animal's neck. The fat boy was plainly asleep. He had been slumbering in the saddle for more than an hour, and occasional mutterings indicated that he was dreaming.

"Professor, don't you think we had better make camp and take a rest?" asked the first boy in the line, addressing the grizzled leader.

Professor Zepplin cast a critical glance down the line of jaded horses and riders, a faint smile twitching the corners of his mouth.

"All tired out, eh, Tad?" he questioned.

"Yes, I'll confess that I am for once. Of course I can stand it as long as the next one, but there's no use in wearing out the stock," answered Tad Butler. "Chunky's asleep. Ned and Walter will be in a few minutes more."

"Very good; call a halt. We will ride into the bushes over there on the other side of the stream. The water cannot be deep. Some hot coffee will wake us all up."

"Hoo - oo!" cried Tad, interrupting the professor. "Wake up, fellows, and make camp!"

"Wha - what's up?" demanded Ned Rector, straightening in his saddle.

"Nothing's up, except ourselves, and we'll all be down in a minute. We're going to ford the stream and make camp on the other side."

"Is this the Guadalupe range?" asked Walter Perkins sleepily.

"This is the loop all right, but not the Guadalupe," laughed Rector. "Hullo, Chunky's in the Land of Nod."

"Wake him up, Ned," nodded Tad.

"Not much. Let him wake himself up."

"His pony has gone to sleep, too," added Walter.

"Yes, they are a couple of sleepy heads, Tad."

As the lads turned to gaze at the fat boy, they could not repress a shout of laughter. Stacy Brown's pony now stood the picture of dejection, its nose clear to the ground. Chunky had settled in his saddle until it seemed that the boy was less than half his natural height. His body had fairly telescoped itself. The fat boy sat leaning forward, his sombrero tipped forward until it covered his face, leaving only the point of the chin exposed.

By this time Professor Zepplin had driven his own pony into the creek, the others following, where the horses drank greedily. Stacy and his mount were still on the bank, too sound asleep to think of either water or food.

"Stacy!" shouted the professor.

"Oh let him sleep," begged the boys.

"Too bad to disturb his infantile slumbers," jeered Ned Rector.

"But he will fall off."

"It wouldn't be the first time," laughed Tad. "Gid-ap!"

The ponies climbed the opposite bank, the tired Pony Riders throwing themselves off and quickly stripping the equipment from their mounts. They then led the animals farther into the bushes, where the ponies were tethered until they should be wanted again.

Chunky still slumbered on.

In the meantime Tad was carrying water from the creek, while the other two boys were starting a fire on the bank, the smoke from which was already curling up lazily into the still, hot air. But not much of a meal was cooked. It was too hot to eat or to cook. The boys sat down to their little meal, almost choking with laughter every time they glanced across the stream toward the sleeping pony and its sleeping rider.

"Most remarkable," nodded the professor. "Surely the smell of food ought to awaken him if nothing else does."

"He's just as much of a sleeper as he is an eater, Professor," declared Rector.

"That would be impossible," objected Tad. "As an eater he is a champion, as a sleeper he is just above the average. You're the champion sleeper of this outfit, Ned."

"It's too hot to resent your unseemly remarks, Tad. I'll take that matter up when we get to the mountains. By the way, how much farther is it to the mountains?"

"Just as far as it was this morning. How about it, Professor?"

"We ought to reach them this afternoon. According to my understanding, we were a little more than forty miles from them this morning. Since then we have gone a good twentyfive miles."

"Then we will camp there to-night?" questioned Walter.

"Yes, I hope so."

"What are we going to do about Chunky?" demanded Walter.

All eyes were directed toward the sleeping fat boy and his slumbering pony. The latter was now beginning to show some signs of life. It had lifted one foot, then another, until it had taken two steps toward the creek. But the rider was as soundly asleep as before. Nothing seemed to disturb Chunky when he was having a nap.

"He will fall off. Wake him up!" commanded the professor.

"Oh, please don't bother him. We want to see what he will do," begged Walter.

"I think you will see, all right," chuckled Tad. "You will see what you shall see, and -"

"There he goes!"

The pony had taken three or four more steps toward the stream. Now its eyes were partly open. It saw the rest of the party on the other side of the creek.

The cool water completed the awakening process for the horse. It drank freely then started for the other side, Chunky still sleeping. All at once the pony stepped into a deep hole in the creek. The animal went down on its nose with a mighty splash. Stacy shot over the disappearing head, then boy and pony vanished under the waters of Delaware Creek while the others of the party bowled with delight.

"Oh, wow!" howled Stacy, coming to the surface and making for shore with mighty splashes, coughs and chokings. "Oh, wow!"

Walter ran down to the water's edge, lending the unfortunate fat boy a helping hand. The pony in the meantime had clambered up the bank and was trotting off to join its fellows.

"What - what - who did that?" demanded Stacy belligerently.

"Did what?" replied Ned.

"Who threw me in?"

"I reckon you threw yourself in," answered Tad.

"I didn't."

"The pony did it for you. Don't be a goose," commanded Ned.

"Yes, you went to sleep. You've been asleep for the last ten miles or so," nodded Butler.

"I'm all wet," wailed Stacy.

"You will be dry in a few moments in this hot sun," interposed the professor.

"I don't want to be dry."

"Then jump in again," suggested Butler. "Anyhow, you've missed your dinner."

"I - I've - what?"

"Missed your dinner."

Chunky's gaze wandered from the camp fire to the dishes and provisions that already were being packed preparatory to moving on.

"I want my dinner," he wailed.

"Dinner is finished, young man," replied the professor severely. "You should be on hand when meals are being served. There is no second table in this outfit, except for good and sufficient reasons."

"My reasons are good. I - I fell in, I did. And - say, why didn't you fellows wake me up?" demanded the fat boy, a sudden suspicion entering his mind. He began to understand that a trick had been played upon him. "What'd you let me sleep for?"

"Because you were sleepy," answered Ned Rector solemnly.

"That's a mean trick. I wouldn't play that on a horse," answered Stacy indignantly.

"But you did play it on a horse," spoke up Tad. "The horse went to sleep with you, out of sheer sympathy I should say."

"I should think he would have. Anything would go to sleep with Chunky on hand," declared Ned.

"You fellows are too funny! I don't care what you think. I'm going to have something to eat. Where's the biscuit?"

"Packed."

"Then we'll unpack them again. I guess I've got as much right to the grub of this outfit as the next one."

With that Stacy helped himself to such of the food as he was able to find. In order to get what he wanted he was obliged to undo three of the large packs. Once undone no one would help him lash them together again, so grumbling and growling, the fat boy tugged with the ropes until he had taken a secure hitch about each of the three packages. They made him tie the three before they would allow him to eat the biscuit and cold bacon that he had got out.

While Stacy was munching his cold lunch the others were lashing the packs to the lazy ponies and preparing to start again, every one being anxious to reach the mountains before night fell. But the fat boy was surly as well as sleepy. He felt aggrieved. That his companions should sit down to a meal, leaving him asleep on his pony, filled Stacy with resentment and a deep-rooted determination to be even with them. He was already planning how he could repay his companions in their own coin.

Frank Gee Patchin

"Better not try it," suggested Tad carelessly as he passed the fat boy on his way to get his pony.

"Try what?"

"To get even," answered Tad laughingly.

"How do you know that I was thinking of such a thing?"

"Perhaps I read your mind."

"Humph! You better learn to read your own before you go prying into mine. I'll show you what I'm going to do."

"Cinch up," interrupted the voice of Professor Zepplin. "We have no time to waste."

Still grumbling, Stacy climbed into the saddle. He promptly fell off, having forgotten to cinch the saddle girth. Now the pony woke up and began to kick as the saddle slipped under its belly. Stacy moved more quickly than he had at any other time during the day. Over and over he rolled in a cloud of dust in his efforts to get out of the danger zone, while the pony kicked and squealed, the boys shouting with laughter.

"Whoa!" roared the fat boy, sitting up after he had reached a place where he considered it safe to do so. "Whoa! Catch him, somebody."

"Catch him yourself," retorted Ned.

Tad's rope wriggled through the air. It caught one of the flying hind feet of the pony. Then the little animal plowed the dirt with its nose, while Walter sprang forward, sitting down on the angry animal's head.

"Now get that saddle off," commanded Tad. "Come, Chunky! Do you think we are going to wait here all day for you?"

The fat boy reluctantly obeyed the command of Tad Butler. After some further trouble, Stacy's pony was properly saddled, but still stubborn and ready for further trouble. The lad got on this time without falling off, and with much laughter and joking, the party started off toward the blue haze in the distance, the dark ridge that marked the Guadalupes.

It was in "*The Pony Rider Boys in the Rockies*" that our readers first learned how this little private club of youthful horsemen came to be organized. The need of open-air life for the then sickly Walter Perkins was one of the great factors in the organization of this little band of rough-and-ready travelers. Our readers remember the adventures of our young friends in the fastnesses of the Rocky Mountains. These lads speedily fitted themselves into the stirring life of the big game land, and had other yet more startling adventures in which wild animals did not play so strong a part as did wild men. The story of the discovery of Lost Claim, with its accompanying battle with claim-jumpers, was fully told in this first volume.

It was in "*The Pony Rider Boys In Texas*" that we found the lads learning the first rudiments of the cattle business. The thrilling part that the young men took in the long cattle drive, with its stampedes, the fording of swollen rivers, the games of the cowboys and the tricks of the cattle thieves, is related in that second volume.

Frank Gee Patchin

How the boys improved their shooting and mastered the details of that fascinating sport of handling the lariat are all familiar to our readers.

In "*The Pony Rider Boys in Montana*" is told the story of the long and exciting ride over the old Custer Trail, famous in the tragic annals of our earlier days of Indian fighting. Here the boys found themselves drawn into the life of the sheep men, on those great ranges where the sheep men must still defend themselves from the prejudices, and sometimes from the extreme violence, of the cattle men. It was in this connection that Tad Butler and his friends discovered leading clues in the great conspiracy of certain cattle men against the prosperity and safety of the sheep men. This state of affairs led finally to an angry battle, at which the boys were present. Then, too, our readers all recall Tad Butler's capture by the Blackfeet Indians, and all that befell him ere he succeeded in escaping to his friends.

The next stage of adventures took our lads somewhat further east, as told in "*The Pony Rider Boys in the Ozarks*." It was a thrilling, desperate time when the boys, with their ponies stolen, found themselves facing actual starvation in the wilds. Tad Butler's perilous trip for assistance is bound to bring throbs of recollection to every reader of that volume. The imprisonment of the youngsters in a mine, following a big explosion, formed another interesting scene in the narrative brought forth in that fourth volume of the series. It was here that Chunky, as our readers know, displayed the splendid stuff that lurked under his odd exterior and behind his sometimes queer manners. How, in escaping from the mine, the Pony Rider Boys penetrated a mystery that had disquieted the dwellers near the

Ozarks for a long time, was one of the most interesting features of the tale.

But such strenuous life proves the mettle of the right kind of young Americans. So, far from being discouraged, or sighing for the comforts of home, we next find our lads in Nevada, as related in "*The Pony Rider Boys on the Alkali*." Here they left grass behind for the glaring discomforts of the baked desert lands, where severe thirst was one of the least yet most constant perils. Roving from water hole to water hole, finding them all gone dry, nearly drove the youngsters mad. Then, too, the fight with the mad hermit, who seemed a part of the life of that bleak desert, helped to accustom the boys to the strenuous life of daily danger.

As our readers will recall, it was in the next volume, "*The Pony Rider Boys in New Mexico*," that the author described the events surrounding the first real acquaintance that our lads formed with the little that is left of the savage Indian to-day. It was here, too, that they beheld the fire dance of the Saboba Indians in all its ancient fury. The adventures of the young horsemen at this point became fast and furious. Between prairie fire and fight they had the most exciting time of their lives.

Later, after a rest at home, as described in "*The Pony Rider Boys in the Grand Canyon*," the boys visited the wonderful region of the Colorado. Here, as our readers will recollect, the lads were cut off from their trail by the falling of great masses of rock during a fierce storm. Apparently the boys were doomed to remain helpless on a narrow shelf of rock; our readers recall how Tad Butler, at the risk of his life, spent hours in the attempt to get them out of their dangerous situation. The mysterious circumstances that followed the boys all the way along on their journey through the great canyon form a most remarkable series of events.

Now, from Arizona, Tad and his friends had journeyed onward and into the Lone Star State. Here they looked forward only to a long, healthful ride, full of pleasures, yet devoid of anything like sensational excitement. Yet one never knows what the day may bring forth, and these young travelers of ours, though they did not suspect it, were on the threshold of the most exciting experiences that had yet befallen them. The blue mountain ridge in the near distance was teeming with the story that was to unfold before them. So far the ride had been lonely. Of late rarely had they come in sight of a building of any sort, for this part of the state was but sparsely settled. To meet a horseman was an event. In fact they had not met one since the early morning. The Pony Riders had no guide with them on this journey, believing that one would not be needed. Nor did they carry a pack train. One additional pony bore all their extra baggage, each mount being loaded with all that he could carry in addition to its rider. For tents they had brought one large enough to accommodate the entire party. This was in sections, carried on the different ponies.

Five o'clock had come and gone. The sun was partly bidden by the ridge of the Guadalupes towards which the Pony Rider Boys were slowly drawing. Ned called up to the professor who was riding at the head.

"Where are we going to make camp, Professor?"

"Tad will decide that," answered Professor Zepplin without looking back.

"Near a stream, of course," answered Butler.

"Any mosquitoes there?" demanded Stacy.

"No odds, if there are," retorted Ned. "They wouldn't bite you."

"Not if they had got at you first," returned Stacy solemnly. "There's a level place in there by the creek."

"I see it. I'll ride on and have a closer look at it."

Butler spurred his pony ahead of the others. Reaching the foothills of the range he shaded his eyes, gazing up into the cool, green valley or canyon that led into the mountains.

"I guess this will do very well, boys," he said. "I -"

Bang!

"Wow!"

Stacy with a howl of terror slid from his pony, sending up a little cloud of dust as he collapsed on the plain.

"Wha - what - what - " gasped the professor.

Bang!

Professor Zepplin's sombrero was snipped from his head. Stacy lay groaning on the ground.

"Ride for the rocks!" shouted Tad as shot after shot began popping from somewhere in the mountains, the bullets screaming over their heads close to their ears or snipping up flecks of dust in the plain.

Tad drove his pony straight at Stacy Brown. He scooped the fat boy up by the collar and rode madly for the protection of the rocks, Chunky's heels dragging on the ground. The others rode madly after them, while the shots were still being fired at them. It was an exciting moment. No one knew what the shooting meant, nor did they know whether Stacy really had been hit or not. There was no time to stop to reason the matter out. It was a case of getting to cover as fast as horse-flesh would carry them.

CHAPTER II

A MYSTERIOUS ATTACK

"Pull in close!" cried Tad.

"Where is it coming from?" shouted Ned.

"I don't know. I haven't had time to look. Look out there!"

Professor Zepplin, somewhat slower than the others, had halted a little distance out from the foothills. A bullet threw up a little cloud of dust just to one side of where he was sitting on his pony, followed by a report somewhere up in the mountains.

"Stop that! Stop it, I tell you!" bellowed the professor, waving his sombrero. Almost ere the words were out of his mouth, the sombrero was shot from his hand and went spinning out to the rear. Professor Zepplin did not wait for further parley. He turned his horse, dashing for the protection of the foothills.

In the meantime, Tad Butler had leaped from his pony, placing Stacy on the ground. It was observed that there was blood on the fat boy's left cheek, but his eyes, wide and frightened, were staring up at the boys now gathering about him.

Frank Gee Patchin

"Are you hurt?" demanded Tad breathlessly.

"I'm killed."

"Nonsense! It's only a flesh wound -"

"Is - is he shot?" stammered Walter Perkins.

"Of course I'm shot. Don't you see I am?" demanded Chunky with considerable spirit for a man who had been the mark of a bullet and who according to his own word was dead.

Tad half dragged the fat boy down to the creek where the blood was quickly washed from his cheek. It was then seen that a bullet had grazed Stacy's cheek, leaving a raw streak across it.

Professor Zepplin, now mindful of his duty, had hurried up to them, and down on his knees was examining the wound critically.

"Hm - m - m!" he muttered. "Bad business, bad business!"

"But - what does it mean?" urged Walter.

"What does it mean? It means that the Germans have got us," wailed Stacy Drown. "Oh, I knew we should be in this war sooner or later, but I didn't think I should be the first man to get shotted up."

"It means some one has been trying to shoot us up," answered Rector.

"Trying!" exploded Chunky. "They did more than try.

They succeeded. Don't you see this wound on my countenance? Wait till I get sight of the man who put that mark on my face. I'll bear the scar for life. I -"

"It is my opinion that we are in a dangerous position," declared the professor, getting up and glancing about him apprehensively.

"We were. We are all right here for a little while," replied Tad. "But we shall have to seek other quarters, I am afraid, and that without delay."

"Surely, it must be a mistake," protested the professor. "Some one must have been shooting at us under a misapprehension that we were another party."

"It doesn't make any difference what their motive is, sir," answered Tad. "The fact remains that some one is trying to get us and we must look lively or they will pink one or more of us. Get up, Stacy! You are all right. Lead your pony in here while I take an observation."

Tad mounted his own horse and galloped along at the base of the rocks, well shielded from any one who might be hiding further back in the mountains. The Pony Rider Boy's mind was working rapidly. He was forming a plan of campaign. He was inclined to agree with the theory of Professor Zepplin. Still, theories would not help them at this critical moment. They must protect themselves and at once if they expected to get out alive. One course was plainly open to them. They could mount their ponies and ride out over the plains at a gallop and perhaps escape. However, this plan was rather risky. Besides, Tad did not like the idea of running away.

"No, we've got to do something else," he declared out loud. "I have it!" The boy brought his pony up standing and gazed off over the plain to a point about a quarter of a mile beyond, where the plain rolled into a hollow, a "hog hollow" as it was called down there.

Butler galloped back to where his companions were standing anxiously awaiting him.

"We are wasting time, Tad," cried the professor as the lad rode up. "It is my opinion that we had better ride into that canyon there and make camp in some secluded spot where we shall not be easily found."

"I am afraid that won't help us any, Professor," said Tad. "How could we expect to hide ourselves in there so completely that a mountaineer would not find us? No, sir, it is my opinion that our only safety lies out there in the open, at least for the rest of the afternoon and the night."

"What, ride out there to be shot up again?" demanded Stacy. "No, sir, not for Stacy Brown! I've been shot up once. I don't propose to make a bull's-eye of myself again."

"Stacy is right, boys. It would be foolishness to follow such a course and -"

"Wait till you hear my plan, sir," urged Butler.

"We will hear it. Proceed."

"Out yonder about a quarter of a mile from the base of the rocks is a depression in the plain. If we can reach it we shall be safe - "

"Yes, if we can reach it," repeated Ned.

"In doing so we should be shot in all probability," objected Professor Zepplin.

"I think not, sir."

"Explain what you mean?"

"From the position occupied by the man or men when they fired at us out there, I am sure they could not see us were we to follow the course I went out on just now. If you will ride down to the edge of the foothills with me and wait there, I will gallop out and prove my theory."

"What do you mean?" questioned the professor.

"I will see if I can draw their fire," answered Tad.

Professor Zepplin shook his head.

"Too risky!"

"It certainly is risky to stay here. Listen, sir. If that man wants to get us he surely will be creeping down on our position before long. We are in greater peril here, where we can't see anything on one side of us, than we would be out there where we have an unobstructed view on all sides. My plan is to make camp out in the hollow; then we will place a guard over the camp, keeping a sharp watch all through the night. By morning we'll be able to find out what is in the wind."
"I won't move a step," declared Stacy stubbornly.

"You will do whatever seems best to the rest of us,"

answered the professor sternly. Then, after a moment's thought, he added, "I am inclined, upon second thought, to agree with Tad. We will try the plan."

"Good. Follow me. Get that pony, Chunky. I told you once before to catch him. We'll be in a fine mess if you lose your mount."

"I'd rather lose my mount than to lose my precious life," answered the fat boy surlily.

By this time the others were taking to their saddles. The faces of all wore serious expressions. They had not looked for anything quite so lively as this. It was not the first time the Pony Rider Boys hadsmelled powder when the powder was being expended on them, but they liked it none the better for past experiences.

Stacy's cheek was bleeding again. He was holding his handkerchief to the wound and his face was a little paler than usual.

"Buck up!" commanded Ned. "You're not going to show the white feather, are you?"

"No, it's a red feather I'm showing," wailed the fat boy.

"Forward!" ordered Butler. "Get up, Chunky!"

The party moved off, keeping close to the rocks, Tad now and then casting apprehensive glances up to their tops. He was not wholly satisfied that they were out of range of the bullets. The man who had been firing at them, too, was practically a dead shot.

"Now spread out," commanded Tad after they bad reached the point where he previously had halted. "Don't shout, but when I wave my hand, ride fast for the hollow. I'll be all right; don't worry about me."

With that the lad galloped leisurely out on the plain, his back to the mountains. It was a bold thing to do. Deep down in his heart the Pony Rider Boy expected every second to bear a bullet scream over his head, providing he was fortunate enough not to stop the bullet with his body. Not a shot greeted his bold act.

Tad rode on, finally disappearing in the "hog hollow." A few moments later he rode up the ridge, waving his hands for them to come on. Professor Zepplin started out at once, followed by the others of his party, Stacy this time well up toward the front of the line. For reasons of his own he did not care to drag behind. If there was to be any shooting he wanted to be as far away from it as possible.

The trip was made at a fast gallop and without incident, the party reaching the hollow without having drawn a shot from the enemy.

"It is my opinion," declared the professor, "that, whoever our cnemy may be, he has discovered that he has made a mistake."

Tad shook his head.

"I don't think we would be safe in taking that for granted. He did not see us, but he will be on hand before long. I'm going back there before he does see us. If he starts any more shooting you all lie low."

"Where are you going?" demanded the professor.

"On a scouting trip."

"I cannot consent to any such foolhardy business," answered Professor Zepplin sternly.

"It is not foolhardy. We've got to clear up this mystery. Don't you see, we shan't dare go any farther - -we simply cannot go into the mountains knowing there is some one there waiting to riddle us the first time he gets a clear sight at us?"

"But what do you propose to do?"

"I don't know, beyond finding out what is up."

"Yes, let him go," urged Stacy. "He's looking for trouble. I'm the only one who has had any experience thus far. It's time some one else made a mark of himself."

"I was thinking of taking you with me," laughed Tad.

"No, you don't! Not if I see you coming," objected Stacy.

"Yes, take him along," urged Ned.

"No, I think I'll take you, the Professor being willing," answered Tad nodding at Rector.

Ned stopped smiling, gazing at Tad to see whether the latter were in earnest. Tad was.

"All right, I'm willing, Tad."

"How about it, Professor?"

"Provided you do not go into the mountains I will agree to your plan. But I cannot consent to your taking further desperate chances."

"I hope you will not hold me to that, Professor."

"To what?" demanded Professor Zepplin shortly.

"To not going beyond the edge of the mountains."

"Plainly, what is it you are planning to do, Tad?"

"I want to find out who it is that is shooting at us and why. That is all, sir."

"You don't suppose it possibly could be the Germans attacking us, do you?" questioned Walter apprehensively.

The professor shook his head.

"If you will stop to think you will see how necessary it is for some one to do something," urged Tad Butler.

"Yes; don't let me do it all," urged Stacy. "I think I have done my share already. It is high time some one else got a move on. First thing we know we shan't know anything. We'll be dead ones, and -"

"Very good. Go on. There will be no peace here unless you have your way. See to it that you are back here in an hour. If not we shall go after you. Do you understand?"

"Yes, sir, I will try to get back on time. If something should occur to keep us longer than that please don't worry. You know we might not be able to get away. If we get into trouble I will signal by firing three shots into the air. Are you ready, Ned?"

"Yes. Do we take our arms?"

"Better leave the rifles here. We don't want to be bothered with them. We'll take our revolvers. That will be sufficient."

"Now, Tad, be prudent," begged the professor. "I know you have a level head or I should not permit you to get out of my sight under the circumstances."

"We will be prudent, sir. Come on, Ned; we mustn't waste a moment now. If we are seen to leave the camp we'll fail."

For answer Ned swung himself into his saddle, after first having taken the rifle from the saddle boot and fastened it to one of the packs.

"Don't pitch the tent yet. We must be in marching order," directed Butler, after leaping into his saddle. "And don't worry about us, for we'll be all right."

Nodding to Ned Tad started off at a fast gallop. But despite Tad's cheerfulness he realized that he had taken upon himself a serious piece of work, one that might be the death of both. Still, he was nothing daunted. He was determined to go to the bottom of the mystery, whatever the cost might be to himself.

Tad knew also that he could depend upon Ned Rector,

for Ned was brave and resourceful, a boy who would keep his head in an emergency.

They made the trip to the mountains without incident. There Tad pulled up for a conference.

"Now tell me what your plan is?" said Ned.

"First we will ride on a little further along the base here. I see a place where I think we can hide our ponies. I don't want to go back to the point where we first started to make camp. That is the place where our enemy will be looking for us first. But when he gets there we'll be somewhere in the vicinity."

Ned wheeled his pony without further comment and followed Tad at a slow trot along the base of the foothills. The boys were engaged on a more desperate mission than they knew.

CHAPTER III

IN A BAD MAN'S POWER

Having secreted their ponies in a dense growth of scrub oak, Tad laid out his plan as follows:

"You, Ned, will go straight in from here until you've got about a quarter of a mile directly inland. When you have done so turn due west. I don't think you can lose your way for you can see out every little while and thus get your bearings."

"Where are you going?"

"Back to the point where we first decided to make camp. I shall have easier going than you will, but I shall be in more risk."

"What's the rest?" asked Ned with a short laugh.

"It is my idea to close in on the right fork of the stream there in the foothills. I'll come up from the west and you from the east. In that way we shall close in, you see, covering roughly the greater part of the territory."

"Then you think we shall find our man there?"

"I am sure he will get there eventually, provided he has

not seen our movements out there. He will go to the stream and from there he will quickly locate our camp. Understand?"

"As far as it goes, yes. But what are we going to do if we find him?"

"Watch him. Find out what he is up to, then from that on be guided by circumstances. But whatever you do, Ned, don't use your revolver unless it be to save your own life."

"No, I'm not aching to shoot any one. Do you know, Tad, I'm thinking you and I are biting off a bigger mouthful than we will know how to chew?"

"We will manage it somehow."

"What do you think this fellow is trying to do?"

"It looked very much as if he were trying to kill us," smiled Tad.

"It did. But what for?"

"I have an idea the professor was right when he said the fellow mistook us for some other party."

"And he's likely to do it again, if that's the case."

"He may have already discovered his mistake, Ned. You observe he hasn't fired a shot since?"

Rector nodded thoughtfully.

"Well, we must be on the move. We don't want to be

caught out here after dark, you know, Ned. Remember, the right fork, where it enters the hills, is the point we have agreed upon meeting. You will strike the stream farther back, then follow it, but be very careful. Be an Indian, Ned. If you are a white man you're likely to lose your identity. We don't want to stop any bullets. Chunky has done quite enough of that for one day."

"I'll watch out - never you fear, old man."

"Then here we go."

Tad crept silently away, hugging the base of the rocks so that it would have been difficult for one at the top to have seen him at all Ned, obeying his instructions, found a canyon up which he crawled, neither boy making a sound. They had agreed upon the two-shot signal to call each other, three shots being a warning to the rest of their party that they were in need of assistance.

Neither lad saw or heard anything of a disturbing nature on his way out. Ned found no difficulty in making his way into the range of mountains, but as he proceeded and found no one there he grew more bold. Not that he was particularly careless, but he unconsciously relaxed a little of his former caution.

In the meantime Tad Butler had crept on past the place where the party had first planned to go into camp. Not a sign of a human being greeted Tad's watchful eyes. The lad climbed the side of the rocks, keeping his body hidden in the foliage as much as possible. He had got about half way up when he paused to take a look over the plain beneath him. The Pony Rider Boy could faintly make out the place where his companions were in camp awaiting the result of his mission.

"I believe there's Chunky standing on that rise," muttered Tad. "Yes it must be Chunky. I'll bet the professor doesn't know the boy is out there. Chunky evidently is getting anxious about us."

Bang!

The shot sounded some distance to the eastward of where Tad was secreted. Instinctively the lad glanced toward the camp again. Stacy Brown no longer was to be seen. Tad Butler could not repress a laugh. He had a pretty clear idea as to what had caused Chunky's sudden disappearance. It did not occur to him that possibly Stacy had been bit. As a matter of fact the unknown marksman's bullet had grazed the head of the fat boy, instilling in that young gentleman a more thorough respect for the mountaineer's marksmanship.

But now Tad's mind turned to the object of his visit to the mountain range. He was there looking for the man who had fired the shot. Ned Rector had heard the shot also. Both boys were making their way toward the spot whence the shot had seemed to come. Ned had located the sound much nearer than had Tad. The latter struck off in a southeasterly direction which carried him still farther into the hills. He had reasoned that the shooter was occupying a high point of vantage somewhere farther in, whence he was taking pot shots at the camp of the Pony Rider Boys. In this Tad was mistaken. The mountaineer was much nearer the plains than Tad thought.

Ned started on a trot immediately after having heard the shot.

"I've got him this time!" exulted Rector. "I've got a chance to show the fellows what sort of a trailer I am. They don't think I'm any good, except Tad, and he knows better."

Tad, as he skulked along, was wondering if Ned had heard the shot and hoping that his companion would make no false moves. Each boy was determined to round up the man who had winged Stacy Brown and narrowly missed killing the others of the party.

Night was coming on rapidly and it behooved the lads to make haste. In the first place they did not know these hills, and, in the second, the professor would become alarmed and come in search of them were their return delayed too long. This was not desirable. It might mean the undoing of the entire party unless Tad and Ned succeeded in rounding up their enemy first.

Ned, in his excitement, had a mishap. While creeping along the upper rim of a galley he stepped on a round stone. Ned fell crashing into a heap of rotting limbs and went floundering from there to the bottom of the incline, making a racket that must have been heard clear out on the plain.

The lad got up, his clothing torn, his face scratched, very much chagrined over his blundering fall.

"I guess I'm not so much of a scout as I thought I was," he muttered. "Chunky could have done no worse and for a blundering idiot he's always held the cup up to the present time. I'm glad no one saw me make such an exhibition of myself. But what if that fellow heard me? No, he couldn't. He is too far away."

In this Ned was wrong. The "man" was not so far away as the Pony Rider Boy thought. The fellow, while watching for another opportunity to shoot, had caught the distant sound of crashing twigs. It might have been a falling tree, it might have been an animal. At any rate it put the fellow instantly on his guard. Lowering his rifle he began skulking in the direction of the racket.

By this time Ned was walking ruefully down the galley looking for a convenient trail up the side to the ridge. Not that he could not have made the ascent anywhere, but that he did not wish to raise any more disturbance than be already had done. At last, finding what seemed to him to be a path, Ned began climbing the side of the galley. Had the boy first taken a survey of the ground at the top of the rise, he might possibly have made a discovery, and then again he might not. Crouched behind a rock was a man. The fellow was fingering his rifle suggestively. Twice he raised it to a level with his eyes and drew a bead on the advancing form of Ned Rector, and as many times lowered it.

The watcher observed that Ned carried no rifle, only a revolver slapping against his thigh in its holster as the boy stumbled on up the mountain side. The mountaineer evidently changed his mind about shooting, for he changed ends with the gun and sat waiting. A few moments later Ned stepped up beside the rock where he stood listening and looking about him. The Pony Rider Boy looked everywhere except in the right place.

Suddenly there was a crackling of twigs behind him. Ned turned just in time to see the figure of a man leaping upon him. The boy went down under the crushing weight, the cry that rose to his lips smothered by a stinging blow in the face. Ned lost consciousness. Everything turned suddenly black about him.

CHAPTER IV

TAD BUTLER MAKES A DISCOVERY

Dusk was already settling over the mountains when Ned Butler fell beneath the powerful onslaught of the mountaineer. Without an instant's hesitation the fellow picked up the boy, starting down the side of the galley with his burden. The man ran along carrying the lad as easily as if he had been a child.

Reaching a secluded spot near the west fork the fellow put his burden down, then built a little fire under a thick growth of pines, whose tops served to break up the smoke and scatter it, thus greatly lessening the chances of discovery.

It was a few minutes later that Ned regained consciousness. His captor, watching him narrowly, had placed Ned against a tree, passed a piece of rope about the boy's body, pinioning his arms to his sides, securing the rope at the other side of the tree. Then the fellow had squatted down with rifle across his knees.

Ned saw a powerfully-built, wiry man, whose lean face and deep-sunken eyes created a most unfavorable impression. Even under more pleasing circumstances this man would have caused Ned to give him a wide berth.

Frank Gee Patchin

Discovering that he had been bound Ned's face flushed angrily. Even then he did not realize that his position was a perilous one.

"You untie me and let me go, or it'll be the worse for you," threatened Rector.

"I reckon I've got you this time," grinned the mountaineer.

"I know you. You're the fellow who has been shooting at us. You will get what is coming to you when my friends find out what you have done to me. What do you think I am anyway?"

"That's what I reckoned to find out," answered the man. "Who be you?"

"That's what I am asking you."

"I reckon I ain't answering fool questions."

"Why did you shoot at us?"

"Did I?"

"You know you did."

"What's your name?" asked the mountaineer, evading the question.

"My name is Rector - Ned Rector."

"Where you from?"

"Missouri."

"What you doing here?"

"Maybe I am traveling for my health," answered Ned with a half sneer. He was not advancing his own cause by his attitude.

"I reckon you'll answer my questions and without putting on any trimmings either," announced the fellow, shifting his rifle around so that the barrel lay along his right leg, the muzzle pointing straight at Ned. The latter was not greatly disturbed at this. He did not think, for a moment, that the man would dare to shoot him. Ned did not realize what a desperate character he was facing.

"I will answer what I choose. You can't make me answer any questions that I don't want to," declared Rector defiantly.

"I reckon you'll change yer mind before I git done with you. Anybody with you?"

"No, not exactly here," answered Ned quickly, a sudden line of conduct occurring to him. "Unfortunately for me, and fortunately for you, I am all alone. But when my friends do find out what has happened you'd better look out. You'll be riddled so full of holes that the wind will sigh through your body as if it were a sieve."

"How's Captain Billy?" demanded the man sharply.

"Captain Billy?" wondered Ned.

"Yes. You needn't pretend you don't know what I'm talking about."

Frank Gee Patchin

"I most certainly do not. Who is Captain Billy?"

"Know Joe Withem?"

"I do not. Some friend of yours, I suppose?"

An angry exclamation escaped the lips of the mountaineer.

"I reckon they're no friends of mine. I reckon, too, that you'll be answering my questions or you'll be hiking for the Happy Hunting Grounds in about ten minutes from now. I haven't got all night to sit here talking with you. I've got to git through with you; then I'm going to finish the rest of your crowd. You fellows thought you'd play a sharp trick on me, eh?"

"You are mistaken. We did not even know of your existence until you began shooting at us. Why did you do that?"

"If you don't know, I reckon you'll have to guess. Bill McKay must think we're easy down here, to try a game like that."

"I'll tell him when I see him," nodded Ned.

"I reckon you won't see him right smart. When I git through with you I'm going to send a bullet through your head. Maybe they'll find you here. If they do they'll know what it means, I reckon."

Ned's face paled slightly. There was that in the eyes of the man before him which, all at once, told Ned Rector that the fellow meant what he said.

"Who do you think we are?" demanded the boy earnestly.

"You're part of the Ranger gang."

"The what?"

"The gang known as the Texas Rangers."

Rector laughed.

"You've got it wrong this time. We are not Texas Rangers. We are known as the Pony Riders and we are out for our health and as good a time as we can have."

"Ye can't fool me. That line of talk don't go down at all I'll tell you what. Bill McKay thought to trap some folks by getting in a bunch that wasn't known down in these parts. I had his little game sized up the minute I set eyes on your bunch. But I'll clip your claws. I'll show McKay that we ain't so easy. Now you out with the whole story. If you tell it straight, I may think about letting you go. If you lie it's the end of you. I'd as lief shoot you full of holes as I would a yellow dog. Now what's your orders?"

"I haven't any orders, I tell you."

"What did Bill McKay reckon you would do down here?"

"I don't know Bill McKay, I don't know any Texas Rangers, and if they are anything like you and your kind, I don't want to know them. But I do want to tell you that if you don't let me go - that if you heap any more insults on me - it is you who will get a bullet through your miserable hide. I'm getting mad, Mr. Man."

"Oho! Ye be, eh?"

"Yes, I am."

"Then I reckon there's only one thing to do to put ye in a better frame of mind," answered the mountaineer, shifting his rifle about suggestively. "Now I'll give ye two minutes to open up and tell all ye know," was the stern announcement.

In the meantime Tad Butler had not been idle. As the reader already knows, Tad had been deceived as to the location of the shot. He had gone a long distance out of his course. After a time he realized this and at once started back toward the plain. It was his intention to make the opening where they had first sought to make camp, as it was there or in that vicinity that he was to meet Ned Rector.

The lad settled down to a trot. Every faculty was on the alert, for Butler was a natural woodsman, added to which was an experience of some two or three years in mountain and on plain until Tad was familiar with many of the tricks of the mountaineer.

Suddenly the boy halted and stood with head thrown back sniffing the air.

"Smoke!" breathed Tad. "There is a fire somewhere near here. That means some one is in camp here. I can't be far from the edge now. I must find out where the fire is."

After a few moments of sniffing the lad decided that smoke lay off obliquely to the right of him. Having decided upon this he started in the direction named, but proceeded with much more caution than before as he did not wish to stumble upon strangers until he had first determined whether they were friends or enemies.

At last he saw a faint flicker of light.

"It's there," muttered the boy. "Now we'll see. I hope nothing has happened to Ned. Still, he would have fired his revolver had he got into trouble. He may be waiting for me down by the creek. But I must find out what's going on here before I take time to look him up. I hope the others don't come and blunder in."

Tad paused in his reflections as the sound of voices reached his ears. Young Butler, crouching low, crept cautiously through the bushes, each foot being placed on the ground as softly as an animal stalking its prey could have done. Not a sound did the young woodsman make. Of course his progress was slow, but it was silent, which was much more to be desired.

Some fifteen minutes elapsed before Tad reached a point where he could get a view of the fire. He was obliged to crawl some three or four rods from that point ere he found a position where he could see the men who were near the fire.

The first to attract Tad's attention was the mountaineer, squatting down with head thrust forward, his rifle held across his chest, the man's hand over the trigger-frame. Butler knew that the first finger of the right hand was toying with the trigger. His glances followed the direction indicated by the muzzle of the weapon. Then

Tad's face flushed hot all over. There, back to a tree, a rope twisted twice about his body sat Ned Rector, defiance in face and eyes. Ned was looking straight at his captor. The situation was strained. To Tad, it was maddening.

"What is it you want me to tell you?" demanded the prisoner.

"I've told you that already. What are your orders?"

"And I have already told you, I have no orders from any one."

"How many are in your party?"

"Five, not including the horses."

"I wasn't asking about the cayuses. Who is in charge of you?"

"You wouldn't know if I told you."

"I'm asking you!"

"His name is Zepplin, Professor Zepplin."

"One of them scientific shooters, eh?"

"I don't know about his being a shooter. He is scientific, all right. But what's that got to do with you and me?"

"Did this - this perfesser get his orders from Bill McKay?"

"I should say not," answered Ned with a mirthless laugh.

"Who was it you was to look up?"

"I don't know what you mean."

"Yes you do. Don't try to make a monkey of me. You'll be willing to answer right smart after I've fanned you with a forty-four. Who is it you and your bunch are after?"

"We are after no one. Can't you understand English?" replied Rector with some heat, "I have told you that we are here on a trip for pleasure and nothing else."

"You said you was here for your health, a little time ago," grinned the mountaineer.

"Well, what if we are?" snorted Ned.

"Nothing only that I'm going to drill you full of holes. The two minutes is about up. You've lied to me pretty near every word you've said. You said you didn't know Bill McKay when I know you do. You've said he hadn't given you any orders. You've -"

"You're crazy," scoffed Rector.

"I reckon if I am that you're more so if you think I am going to gulp down all them fairy stories. You're young. Mebby you don't know the kind of a game you've stacked up against, but -"

"I ought to have some idea about it by this time," returned Ned.

"Everything you have said is a lie and you know it. I don't know you, nor do I want to, being somewhat particular about the people I know. And now once more, are you going to let me go?"

A sudden note of triumph had leaped into the tone of Ned Rector. Ned had seen something that sent the blood coursing through his veins madly. That something was a figure that for a few seconds had been outlined in the faint light of the fire.

The mountaineer caught the change of tone on the instant. His suspicions were aroused. His eyes narrowed. He slowly straightened up until he had risen to his full height. Now the rifle came up to position, ready for work. It was at his chest again. The mountaineer had no need to bring the weapon to a level with his eyes. He could shoot equally well from almost any position.

Rector shot a quick glance over the mountaineer's shoulder. He could not resist one more look in Tad's direction. But that look was fatal. With a roar the fellow wheeled like a flash.

Bang, bang!

The shots were fired with such suddenness that Ned did not realize the fellow had turned until after the rifle had spit two charges of fire and lead. Ned's head dropped. Everything grew black about him again. The lad was in a fainting condition. It was all up with him now.

Ned had tried to cry out, but the words would not come. He could not utter a sound if his very life depended upon so doing.

Ned found his voice at last. It rose in a mighty yell for help, a yell that carried far beyond the spot where those exciting scenes were being enacted.

CHAPTER V

WHEN THE TABLES WERE TURNED

At the instant when Ned had shot his quick glance at the wondering Tad, the latter with quick instinct, realizing that Ned had made a serious mistake, threw himself flat on the ground.

That move undoubtedly saved Tad Butler's life. At least, two bullets went ripping through the foliage over his head. The move served the further purpose of hiding him from the man who was shooting at him. The mountaineer had not even caught a sight of Butler, quick as had been his turn about. The fellow swung to the right letting go two more shots, evidently believing that he had not fired in the right direction.

In Tad Butler's right hand was gripped a piece of rock that he had grabbed when he threw himself to the ground. The boy came to his feet as if propelled by a spring. At that second the eyes of the mountaineer were fixed on a point several yards to the left of Tad.

Without a sound Tad let go the rock. But the movement caught the eyes of the ruffian. He swung toward Butler at the same instant pulling the trigger of his rifle.

Once more the rifle roared its savage protest. But that was its last roar for the time being. Almost at the instant when he pulled the trigger the mountaineer received Tad's rock in the pit of his stomach. With such force had the missile been hurled that the fellow staggered back, the rifle falling from his hands, both of which were suddenly clasped over the part of his anatomy that had been struck.

The fellow uttered a howl of pain. He swayed and staggered then fell over a dead limb, landing flat on his back with a crash.

Tad, without an instant's hesitation, sprang forward. The eyes of the plucky Pony Rider Boy were flashing. Tad had not even thought to draw his revolver. But his anger was kindled. He was dangerous in his present mood. He did not pause to think what a terrible chance he was taking in thus rushing forward. Fortunately for Tad, however, the mountaineer was suffering such agonies that he either gave no thought to the revolver that was hanging at his side, or else he was too weak to draw it. He staggered to his feet, swaying, groaning, shoulders hunched forward, chin on his breast.

Young Butler was upon him like a whirlwind.

Whack!

Tad's fist caught the mountaineer squarely on the point of the jaw as the man raised his head half defiantly, one hand groping awkwardly for his pistol.

The fellow went down in a heap.

"Whoop!" howled Ned Rector. "That's the blow that

put the finishing touches to father. Cut me loose! Cut me loose! Quick, Tad! He'll be up in a minute!"

Butler had no need to be told this. He knew the first thing to be done was to secure the prisoner. Ned could wait. The danger lay with the man stretched out there on the ground. Tad worked rapidly. His rope was jerked free from his belt. Three swift turns were made about the body of the prostrate man, binding the fellow's arms firmly to his sides.

Next Tad jerked the mountaineer's revolver from its holster and cast it into the bushes. Then he tied the man's ankles together, after which he straightened up and wiped the sweat from his face and forehead.

"Whew! Warm, isn't it, Ned?"

"Rather," drawled Rector. "Warmer for some folks than others. It came near being pretty warm for you. Are you going to cut me loose, or am I to stay tied to this tree for the rest of the night?"

"I guess we will let you up now. We shall have to wait until our friend there comes to his senses before going farther. Tell me how you got into this mess."

"The same way Chunky gets into trouble. I blundered into it." Ned then went on to relate briefly how he had been jumped on by the mountaineer and made prisoner.

"What was he trying to get you to tell him?"

"He accused me of being a Texas Ranger, a member of some fellow's band, a fellow named McKay."

"The band or the man?" questioned Tad.

"That was the man's name. Billy McKay. He's a captain of Rangers, or something of the sort, it doesn't matter much what."

"I rather think it does," answered Butler dryly.

"How so?"

"Why, don't you see, it means that if the Texas Rangers are after this fellow he must be wanted for something very serious. Who is he?"

"You may search me. Stacy may be right after all. There are plenty of Germans in Mexico, so why not some of them up here to stir up trouble? He looks like pictures I have seen of some of those Hun assassins," declared Ned Rector.

"I think I will search him. He may have some more weapons about his person."

Tad found a bowie knife in the mountaineer's boot, but that was the only weapon left on his person. Tad threw the knife away. About this time the prisoner began to show signs of returning consciousness.

"You must have hit him an awful wallop," wondered Ned, standing over the man and eyeing him narrowly.

"I did. I hit him first with a stone, then with my fist. I skinned my knuckles, too."

Ned grunted.

"I'd hate to have you land on me that way. That surely was a sockdolager. He has his eyes open."

"Oh, hullo!" greeted Butler. "We rather turned the tables on you, didn't we?"

"I'll kill you for this!" growled the prisoner hoarsely.

"I don't think you will kill anybody to-night. What I would like to know is what you mean by trying to shoot us up."

"I'll shoot up the rest of you before I get through with you, you and your whole gang. You can tell Bill McKay what I say and -"

"We don't know Bill McKay. We have nothing to do with any of you people down here. We are here for pleasure."

"That's what the other cayuse said. Looks like you wuz, hey?"

"You alone are to blame for present conditions. We were not looking for you. You began shooting at us before we got into the foothills. Who were you shooting at the last time? I mean before you tried to pot me just now."

A growl was the only answer.

"The question is, what are we going to do with this fellow, Tad?" asked Ned. "Surely it won't be safe to let him go, and we can't leave him here to starve to death."

"No. I'll tell you what. We will fix up a litter - by the

way, fellow, are there any more of your kind fooling about here?"

"You'll find out whether there are or not," grunted the prisoner.

"Thank you. You have answered my question. I now know you are alone. Ned, can you cut down a couple of saplings?"

"Where do you want to carry him?"

"Down to the fork."

"Then let's drag him. Dragging is good enough for that ruffian -- too good for him. He ought to be shot, then rolled down the hill."

"Don't be bloodthirsty. Prisoners of war should be treated with the utmost courtesy and consideration. I guess perhaps we had better not take the time to make a litter. We can carry him down to the fork. Take hold of the feet. I'll take the heavier end. And you, fellow! You will get along much better if you keep quiet. Remember, no yells nor struggles, else I shall be obliged to put you to sleep as I did a short time since. Do you understand?"

There was no reply to the question.

"All right. Pick him up, Ned," directed Tad.

"Are you going to take his rifle?"

"Yes, I guess perhaps it would be best. The rifle is good evidence," decided Butler.

Tad strapped the weapon to his own back. He did not bother to pick up the revolver or the bowie knife. The rifle was the evidence that he wanted to take with him. Then they gathered their prisoner up. He proved a heavy burden, though fortunately the distance was short to the fork where Tad had decided to carry the man. The fellow had nothing to say, but the expression in his eyes made up for what his lips did not utter. The two boys were glad enough when finally they reached their destination and dropped their burden, though none too gently at that.

"Now what?" demanded Ned.

"I want you to hurry over to where the ponies are tethered, then ride to the outfit. Tell them to pack up and move over here at once."

"Give me a signal before you come into the gulch here. I'll answer it if all is right. Then you may come in without fear."

"What are you going to do?"

"I am going to stay here to keep our friend company. He might get lonesome if we were to leave him alone," chuckled Tad. "Get back as soon as you can. I'll have a fire built, then we'll get supper. Did you know this fellow took another shot at Chunky?"

"No. Was that what he shot at?"

"That was it."

"I hope he didn't hit him."

"I guess not."

"Chunky seems to be getting more than his share of lead to-day," answered Rector with a chuckle. "Serves him right. It'll teach him to be more prudent."

"I don't think you are exactly in the position to say much yourself," replied Tad, his eyes twinkling mischievously.

Ned flushed to the roots of his hair.

"For goodness' sake, don't tell the crowd how I got jumped on. I am as easy as a baby. I'll never call myself a mountaineer again."

"Never mind. You showed your grit at any rate. You didn't appear to be the least bit scared."

"I wasn't. But honest, Tad, now that I've had time to think it all over, I'm scared stiff right this minute. I believe he would have shot me."

"There is no doubt of it in my mind. So he thinks we are Rangers?"

"Who arc the Rangers, anyway?"

"The Rangers are a body of men who did much toward clearing this state of the bad men that infested it for a long time."

"They don't seem to have got them all," replied Rector.

"No, there are some near the border still. The Rangers are a sort of police who range over the state wherever their services may be needed. I understand they are paid by the state. I guess there are not many of them left. The necessity for Rangers is not what it was a few years ago."

"So I should judge from what has just happened," answered Ned somewhat ironically.

"Come, are you going to get started tonight?" demanded Tad with a laugh.

"I'm off this very minute."

Ned hurried away laughing. He bore evidences of his recent encounter with the mountaineer, but all this was forgotten now that the man had been taken and was safely tied up back there in the canyon with the ever vigilant Tad Butler on guard over him.

A short time after that Ned was riding his pony over the plain toward the camp at a fast gallop. He shouted as he neared the camp, where no fire had been lighted, uttering a subdued whoop as he rode in. Chunky and the professor met him a few rods from the camp.

"I - I got shot again!" cried Chunky.

"Where is Tad?" called the professor.

"Over on the fork waiting for us. You are to pack up and return with me at once."

"But - but, the danger," protested Professor Zepplin.

"The danger is past. I don't believe you will have to worry."

"Explain what you mean!"

"I'll leave that for Tad to do after we get over there. Are you all ready?"

"Is Tad all right?" demanded Perkins.

"Fit as a fiddle. You can't put Tad out of business for any length of time. You are to fetch everything. We are going into camp where we originally planned to spend the night," advised Rector.

The professor, very much relieved to learn that the boys had met with no harm, but still somewhat nervous from the hours of fretting he had passed when the lads failed to return, now hastened to get ready to accompany Ned. On the way he explained bow Stacy Brown had been fanned by another bullet when the fat boy indiscreetly showed himself on the rise of ground between the camping place and the foothills ofthe mountains.

"Maybe you'll learn something one of these days," scoffed Ned.

"I - I've learned something to-day."

"Have you?"

"I have."

"Well, what have you learned?"

"That these fellows down here can shoot to beat the band."

"I have observed something of the same sort myself," muttered Ned, with the memory of the mountaineer's bombardment of Tad Butler.

The party had set out at a slow trot with Ned leading the way. Ned's confidence assured them that all was as it should be, but the young man turned a deaf ear to all their questions, replying only now and then with the remark that Tad would tell them all that was to be told when they got to the camping place.

In the meantime Tad had built up a fire, mainly for the reason that he wanted to keep his prisoner well in sight all the time. Butler knew that the man was a tough customer and that were he to get free it would be a sad night for Tad Butler, and so, too, perhaps, for the rest of the party.

The prisoner had nothing to say, nor did Butler seek to draw the fellow into conversation. But the man was watching every move of the young rider who had so cleverly outwitted and captured him. The mountaineer now believed more firmly than before that these two young men were carrying out the orders of Captain Billy McKay of the Texas Rangers. He swore to be revenged on every man of them when once he had gained his freedom. At present that hour of revenge was a long way off.

Suddenly a loud "Yip! Yip! Yahee!" sounded off on the plain. Tad smiled broadly.

"That's Stacy Brown, I'll wager my hat. I'll bet Ned is scolding him, too."

Ned was. He was at that instant threatening to break

Chunky's head if he opened his mouth again before they reached the camping place. Shortly after that Butler's keen ears caught the sound of hoofbeats. He stepped back into the shadows, the prisoner eyeing him inquiringly. Tad did not take the trouble to explain. Let the prisoner think what he might. Then the party rode in in single file. Tad was not in sight. He was hiding in the bushes.

Professor Zepplin pulled up short when his glances finally came to rest on the bound form of the mountaineer; Stacy Brown's eyes grew large and Walter Perkins gasped.

CHAPTER VI

THE CAMP IN AN UPROAR

"Tad! Where is Tad? What does this mean?" demanded the professor.

"Hullo, boys," cried Butler stepping out into the light. "Did you think that was myself tied up there?"

Chunky, in the excitement of the moment, forgot to tell Tad that he had stopped another bullet out on the plain.

"What do you think of our prisoner, Professor?"

"Tad, will you be good enough to explain what this means?"

"Yes, sir. To be brief that's the fellow who shot at us. He tried to kill us both up here in the mountains."

"Are you sure?"

"Positive."

"I guess I ought to know," grinned Rector, "He jumped me, tied me to a tree, then was about to blow my head off when Tad appeared just in time to save my precious life."

By this time Stacy had slipped from his saddle and striding over to the prisoner stood looking down at him. "So, you're the fellow who potted me twice to-day, are you?" demanded the fat boy sternly. The prisoner made no reply, but he gazed up at his tormentor so savagely that Stacy instinctively took a step backward.

"He is the man, but we landed him," answered Rector proudly.

"Is there any objection to my giving the ruffian a good hard kick for luck?" asked Stacy.

"There certainly is objection to your doing anything of the sort," returned Tad sharply. "We have not come to the point where we treat our prisoners of war the way the Germans do theirs. You let the man alone or I'll have something to say to you."

"Stacy!" rebuked Professor Zepplin sternly.

"Yes, sir?"

"You will keep away from the prisoner. Tad, I want to hear all about this."

"There is not much to tell, except that we got him, though he nearly got us. He caught Ned napping. I should have fallen just the same had I been in Ned's place, for this fellow is a bad man. Ned has told you what happened to him, else I shouldn't have said anything about that part of the affair. While Ned was trying to find where the shot came from that caught Stacy last, this fellow spotted and captured him. I was hunting for the source of the shot at the same time, but went astray. I was finally attracted by the smell of smoke. I arrived on the scene about the time that fellow was getting ready to take Ned's life. At least, that was the way it seemed to me."

"Yes, he was," interjected Rector.

"You were an easy mark!" jeered Stacy.

"At least I didn't stop two bullets," answered Ned witheringly.

"The fellow caught Ned looking at me and knowing instantly that something was wrong he whirled and shot at me. He missed, then I shied a stone into his solar plexus," said Tad.

"That sounds like astronomy," ventured Stacy.

"You're wrong; it's geography," chuckled Rector. "I'll finish the story. The ruffian fired twice more after the first two shots at Tad; then he went down as the stone landed on him. By the time he had got up, Tad was on the job and punched him in the jaw."

"Boys, boys!" rebuked Professor Zepplin. "One would think this was a prize fight you were describing."

"It's the truth," protested Ned.

"Of course it is," laughed Tad.

"That may be. But be good enough to moderate your language. You can describe the scene without using questionable language."

"Yes, it's disgraceful," added Stacy, whereat Ned gave the fat boy another withering look.

"As I was about to say," continued Rector, "this gentleman of the mountains had got to his feet when Tad gently smote said gentleman on the tender part of his chin. The gentleman fell down and went to sleep like a little child after a full meal. When the gentleman woke up we had him hog-tied -"

"During which time our friend Ned remained tied to a tree," chuckled Butler.

"Pshaw! I thought so," grunted Stacy. "Brave man is Ned Rector! If you were a scarred veteran like myself then you'd have a right to swell out your chest," added the fat boy, gingerly stroking the bullet mark on his cheek. "Well, go on. We're listening."

"That's all there is to tell, Professor, except that we carried the man down here and there he is."

Professor Zepplin stroked his bristling whiskers reflectively.

"What is your name, my man?" he asked stepping up to the prisoner.

But the fellow made no reply.

"I said what is your name?" repeated Professor Zepplin.

"What's that to you, old Whiskers?"

The professor started, a faint touch of color showing

under his tan, while audible chuckles might have been heard from the boys in the background.

"Such language will not help you. What is your name?"

"Yours will be Mud when I git out of this, you old scarecrow! Don't you stand there jawing over me. I don't like it," added the prisoner, so savagely that the professor shrank back a little.

"It's no use to question him, professor," spoke up Tad. "He won't answer questions."

"I question our right to hold him," said Professor Zepplin. "We have no proof that he is the man who shot at us."

"I've got proof that he assaulted me," bristled Ned.

"And I that he shot at me four times," added Tad. "I should think that were proof enough. What would you do, Professor?"

"I was thinking that we should let the man go with an admonition."

"No, no, no," protested Chunky. "I don't want to be shot up again to-day."

"Don't be afraid, little boy," urged Rector. "We are not going to let the man go - not if I have to fight for it."

"Professor, this fellow thought us Rangers," began Tad.

"Rangers?"

"Yes. He admitted in his questioning of Ned that he thought we were Rangers, or that we had been employed by the Rangers to run him down. That is why he sought to kill us."

"But surely you assured him we were not," protested Professor Zepplin.

"Little stock did he take in our assurances," scoffed Ned. "You might as well talk to the wind."

"But what are we going to do with him, boys?"

"I have thought of that," replied Tad. "It is my idea that he is a bad man. He must be, else the Rangers would not be looking for him. He has proved that he is a dangerous customer to be at large -"

"Yes, he's large, all right," mumbled Stacy. "As I was saying, it seems to me to be our duty to turn him over to the officers of the law."

"Where?"

"I don't know. Is there any town near here?"

"Some twenty miles to the southeast, I believe," answered the professor.

"Then that is where we must take him."

"We may find, then, that we have made a mistake," objected the professor, still doubtful about the wisdom of the course proposed by Tad Butler.

"Then we will make a complaint against him ourselves," answered Tad firmly. "I don't propose to let him off after what he has done. Why, were we to let that man go our lives wouldn't be worth a cent. He would shoot us before the night was over. No, Professor, he must be held prisoner until we can get him to town."

"But we can't go on to-night."

"No. The morning will be time enough. We will give him some food."

"Let me feed the animal," urged Stacy.

"You have steady business performing that office for yourself," retorted Ned Rector.

"In the morning we will take him to town. Shall we get some supper now?"

"Yes. I will think over your proposal in the meantime. Stacy, you might gather some more wood for the fire. Ahem! This has been a most remarkable proceeding all the way through."

"You would have thought so if that fellow had jumped on you as he did on me," growled Ned Rector. "I thought the mountain had fallen down on me. He is bad medicine."

Tad by this time was getting out the things for supper. They were late with this meal owing to circumstances over which they had not had full control, though matters were now pretty well in the hands of the Pony Rider Boys.

"You had better tell us who and what you are. You have heard what has been said here, my man," said the professor returning to the prisoner.

"I reckon I've heard enough. I reckon, too, that you've made a mistake. I ain't what you think. I'll tell you, now that the fresh young feller isn't listening."

"Do so," urged Professor Zepplin, preparing to listen.

"Lean over so the others won't hear."

"Surely."

"You're a right smart old party and I don't mind talking to you, for you've got right smart sense and you'll understand what I'm getting at."

"Say what you have to say, my man. I am listening."

"Between you and me I'm an officer. I'm looking for some parties that have been cutting up didoes down in these parts of late. When I saw your party I thought you were the lawbreakers, so I up and let go. I saw that there were too many for me and it was the only chance I had to -"

"But surely you didn't have to kill us."

"I didn't kill you, did I?"

"True; true."

"I was telling you, I thought you were they and I let go a few shots, just as a tickler. You see, I could have picked you off one at a time just as easy as eating pie.

I'm a dead shot, I am."

"Then you only sought to drive us off?" questioned the professor.

"Yes, that's it. You're a wise old party. They're a bad lot, you know."

"But what about this assault on my boys?" demanded the professor.

"Same thing. I thought they were them."

"Your grammar is shocking, my man, but what you say is deserving of careful consideration. You say you took us to be bad men?"

"Sure I did."

"Who did you think we were?"

"Tuck O'Connor and his crowd."

"Who are they?"

"Well, you see, they do some smuggling over the Rio Grande. Then again, they are up to a few other tricks that the public hasn't got on to yet. What I want to do is to get away from here, quiet-like, so the youngsters won't get wise in time to cut up. Of course I ain't afraid of them. I don't want to hurt them, you see."

"I see," observed the professor dryly.

"I've got to get away to-night. If I'm held till morning I'll have to take you all in. You'll all have to go back with me to State Line and you'll be locked up for interfering with an officer."

"How comes it that you feared we were Rangers then, if this be true?"

"Aw, I was jest bluffing. I wanted the youngsters to give theirselves away, you see."

"I see," reflected the professor.

"Then you'll let me out?"

"I am afraid I can't do that."

"Then lean over here and I'll tell you a secret that'll make you change your mind."

The professor leaned closer. The man's hands, free from the wrists, were moving cautiously. All at once Professor Zepplin's revolver was snipped from its holster and a bullet tore through his clothes, taking some of the professor's skin with it. The professor fell back, staggering to one side out of range where he sank down to the ground holding a hand to his side.

CHAPTER VII

RECEIVING A LATE VISITOR

So unexpected had been the shot that, for a few seconds, the boys stood dumbfounded.

"I'm shot! I'm shot!" yelled the professor.

Bang!

A bullet whistled close to the head of Tad Butler. Stacy Brown, who was just coming into camp with an armful of dry wood for the campfire, dropped his burden and with a howl made for shelter. Tad and Ned had sprung to one side so as to be out of range, while Walter Perkins had flattened himself on the ground.

"Lie still!" commanded Tad sternly as the professor started to get up from where he had sunk down. "Are you much hurt?"

"I - I don't know."

"Drop that pistol, you!" commanded Tad, glowering at the prisoner.

The man laughed.

"I've got you children now," he sneered. "I'll pick you off unless you do as I tell you. Now you come over here. Walk straight, one hand out. Leave your guns behind. Cut me loose or you're a dead one," commanded the prisoner.

"Oh, am I?"

Tad glanced around to make sure that all the boys were out of range. Then with a quick leap he got entirely out of range of the revolver in the hands of the prisoner. Tad had thought he was out of range before, but the man on the ground had twisted the weapon about until its muzzle was pointing in Butler's direction.

But this time the lad got out of range without question. But he was no better off than before. Reaching for his revolver he made the discovery that he had thrown off his belt with revolver and cartridges before beginning to get supper. The others were in no better shape. Not a boy had his revolver on, and the professor's weapon was in the hands of the prisoner.

"I know a trick. I've played it once to-day and I can play it again," declared Tad, searching for a stone, while the others got well out of the way, watching T. Butler. In an emergency they always looked to him to get them out of their difficulties.

"Professor, you lie still. Don't move. I'll fix this fellow. You had better get a good bit farther off," advised the lad, observing a movement on the part of the mountaineer.

Suddenly the latter braced his head and digging his heels into the ground ran around, pivoting on his head.

Tad anticipated the movement by running a few seconds in advance. For a few moments it was a race of wits. The lad as yet had not found a stone suited to his immediate requirements. He was using his eyes in this direction as well as watching the prisoner. Once the latter tried a shot at the boy. The bullet passed Butler rather too close for comfort, but the Pony Rider Boy appeared not to have heard the shot.

Not a word was being said by the lad's companions. The professor lay where he had fallen, the perspiration streaming from his face and body up the side of the canyon the big eyes of Chunky might have been seen peering through between the bushes at the exciting scene below. All at once Tad stooped over. When he straightened up with a bound that carried him several feet to one side, he held a good-sized stone in his right hand.

"Now will you drop that pistol?" demanded the Pony Rider Boy.

"I'll drop you!" roared the enraged enemy.

No sooner had he uttered the words than Tad, with a well-directed toss, dropped the stone fairly on the stomach of the man on the ground.

The prisoner uttered a yell that might have been heard a quarter of a mile away. Ere the yell had died out another stone landed nearly in the same place. The weapon dropped from the hands of the fellow, falling between his legs where he could not reach it without changing his position materially. This he tried to do in a series of quick twists and wriggles, though the boys knew from the expression on his face that he was suffering great pain. It was not surprising, in view of the fact that two rocks, each weighing from eight to ten pounds, had been dropped on his stomach.

The fellow found no opportunity to recover the lost weapon. Tad was upon him with a rush. Grabbing the mountaineer's feet he dragged the man roughly to one side.

"I guess that will be about all for you, my man. You may push us too far. I shan't promise to let you off so easily if you try any more tricks. Professor, are you much hurt?"

"I - I don't know. I'm bleeding."

"Let's see what he did to you."

A quick examination developed the fact that the professor had sustained merely a flesh wound. It was bleeding very little now. Tad, at the professor's direction, washed and dressed the wound, binding a piece of cloth firmly about the waist.

"There, I guess you will be all right now. You may come down, Chunky. The fun is all over for the present. How did he happen to get you that way, Professor?"

Professor Zepplin explained how the prisoner had tricked him, declaring his belief in Tad Butler's statement that the prisoner was a bad man. The professor no longer urged the release of their prisoner. Tad smiled mirthlessly. Perhaps it was better that the professor should have had an object lesson. He would take no further chances with the fellow after that. As for the prisoner, he was fairly frothing at the mouth with rage.

Now that the excitement had come to an end for the moment Stacy Brown went about his task of gathering more wood for the fire. This time he went quite a distance down the canyon, carrying a torch that he might the better find that for which he was in search.

Stacy was busy gathering wood, muttering to himself as was his habit, when all of a sudden he straightened up, conscious that some one was standing beside him. As he rose the fat boy's nose nearly bumped into the muzzle of a revolver. The revolver was backed by a not unpleasant, but stern face.

"Wha - wha - what -" stammered the fat boy. "Wh - wh - who -"

"Not a sound, young man, if you value your life. Who and what are you?"

"I - I'm a Pu - Pu - Pony Rider Boy."

"A what?"

"A Pu - Pony Rider Boy."

"What are you doing here?"

"Ga - gathering firewood."

"Who is your party?"

"Pro - professor Ze - Zep - Zepplin and the boys," stammered the fat boy, trembling at the knees. "I haven't done anything, but I'm a bu - bu - bad man when I get ma - mad."

The stern-faced stranger grinned appreciatively.

"You are not the fellows who came in at State Line the other day, are you?"

"Ye - yes, we're the bu - bu - bunch."

"Oh, fudge!" groaned the stranger. "And to think I've been to all this trouble to round up a bunch of tenderfeet." The man thrust his revolver into its holster with a grunt of disgust.

"I'm Withem," he snapped.

"So am I," answered Chunky.

"I said, 'I'm Withem,'" repeated the stranger.

"I said I was too," reiterated the fat boy.

"Look here, what are you trying to get at, young man?" demanded the newcomer with a slight show of irritation. "Are you trying to make sport of me?"

"N - n - no. You said you were with them - with us - with the crowd, you know. And I said I was too."

The stranger tilted back his head and laughed softly.

"You little cayuse, my name is Withem. W - I - T -H - E - M!" he spelled.

"Oh!"

A broad smile grew on the face of the Pony Rider Boy as he asked:

"What do you reckon you want here?"

"I'm just looking around a bit. I think I'll go to your camp with you."

Stacy surveyed his companion critically from head to foot.

"All right," he said. "If you want to take the chance, I'm willing."

"What chance?" demanded the stranger.

"Tad Butler might take it into his head to throw you out, or something, if he doesn't like your looks."

"I'll take the chance."

"All right; come on. But mind you, it'll be the worse for you if you try to start anything. We're a bad lot, we are, and don't you forget it."

A moment or so later the Pony Rider Boys were amazed to see Stacy strutting in with a stranger in tow.

"He's with us fellows," was the fat boy's announcement.

"Withem's my name," corrected the stranger.

"Yes, he's with 'em. But he hasn't said who it is he is with. I thought I was with him when he shoved a pistol under my nose."

"Good evening, sir," said Tad stepping up, directing a quick, keen glance of inquiry into the eyes of the newcomer. In that one glance Butler decided that the man was all right. It was a relief to see a face like that after their experience with the mountaineer.

As for the prisoner himself, who lay back in a shadow now, he started violently the instant he beheld the man who had just come into the camp of the Pony Rider Boys. The prisoner looked as if he had a severe case of ague for he fairly shrank within himself.

"You are just in time to join us for a bite, Mr. Withem. That is your name, is it not?"

"That's my name."

"Mine is Tad Butler. This is Professor Zepplin. The young man with whom you came in is Stacy Brown, otherwise Chunky, and here are Mr. Rector and Mr. Perkins. If you will gather around the fire I'll serve the chuck."

"Thanks, young man. You certainly know how to do the honors, as well as how to fry bacon. I could smell that across a county and I'd ride to it as fast as horseflesh could carry me."

"Are you from these parts?" asked the professor after they had seated themselves on the ground.

"Yes, I'm from everywhere," laughed Withem. "By the way, young man, that looks like the mark of a bullet on your cheek," he continued, bending a keen glance on Stacy.

"Then it looks like what it is," muttered the fat boy.

"I don't want to be inquisitive, but -"

"No, it isn't considered good manners to be too curious down in this country, I've heard."

"Right you are, yonnker," laughed Withem, in which the others joined heartily. "Men have been known to get into trouble by being too curious, especially down on the Rio Grande. The -"

The visitor's conversation was interrupted by something falling over from beside the tree against which he was sitting. That something was the rifle the boys had taken from the prisoner.

Withem picked up the gun with the purpose of replacing it. He was just standing it against the tree when suddenly he stopped, bringing the gun around in front of him where he could get a better view of it.

The Pony Rider Boys were regarding him questioningly, Tad almost suspiciously. Chunky was wondering if their visitor was going to shoot. The fat boy was ready to run at the first sign of trouble. He had stopped enough bullets for one day. As for the prisoner, his bloodshot eyes were taking in every movement of the man Withem.

"You seem to be much interested," suggested Tad.

Withem flashed a keen, searching look into Butler's face.

"I am."

"Why that's -" began Walter, then subsided at a warning look from Tad.

"Pardon me, but will you be good enough to tell me where you got this rifle? I have good and sufficient reasons for asking the question," said Withem almost sternly.

"We took it from a man who had set out to shoot us up, sir," replied Butler.

"Tried to shoot you up? When? Where?" demanded the visitor with a trace of excitement in his tone.

"This afternoon and to-night. Stacy Brown's cheek bears evidence of the fellow's marksmanship. It seems the man took us to be officers - Rangers, he said."

"Then you - you talked with him?"

"We did," answered Tad with a twinkle in his eyes. "In fact we held quite a lengthy conversation with the gentleman."

"Explain what you are getting at." Withem was deeply interested in the scant information that had been given to him. They saw that he was containing himself with difficulty.

"Tell, Mr. Withem. Don't beat about the bush," advised the professor.

"Yes; tell me what became of the fellow who shot you up," urged the visitor.

"What became of him, sir?"

"Yes, yes!"

"Why we caught and made him prisoner."

"What!"

"Yes, sir, and we have him now," smiled Tad Butler.

"You've got him now? Where is he?" roared the visitor springing to his feet, permitting the captured weapon to fall to the ground.

"He is over there in the bushes," said Tad. "However, I think you had better wait until I get over there before you pay him a visit. I have a sort of proprietary interest in that fellow and I don't propose to have any monkey business. He nearly killed Professor Zepplin, bound though he is. Wait one moment, please. Why do you wish to see the man?"

"Because I think I know him. Gentlemen, I am a Ranger. I am Lieutenant Joe Withem, and I have good reasons to believe your prisoner is a man whom I have been anxious to meet for some time. I am ready to be shown."

Tad wonderingly led the way over to their captive, the lieutenant following in quick, nervous strides, the others of the party bringing up the rear, Chunky lugging a rifle which he kept in position for instant use in case the stranger should seek to liberate their prisoner. But there was little danger of Lieutenant Joe Withem doing anything of the sort,

CHAPTER VIII

A MUCH-WANTED DESPERADO

Tad had snatched a burning brand from the fire, carrying it along with him so that Withem might get a good look at the prisoner. The lad considered it a fortunate coincidence that the Ranger lieutenant should have visited their camp at that particular time.

The instant Withem set eyes on the prisoner he uttered an exclamation under his breath, while the prisoner glared up at him with menacing eyes.

"Hullo, Dunk," greeted the Ranger. "You seem to be in limbo. I reckon you bit off more'n you could chew, for once in your life. Thought you were shooting up Rangers, did you? Instead you barked up against some tenderfeet who were too much for you. I guess you ain't quite so smart as you thought you were."

"I reckon you've made a mistake," growled the prisoner. "I don't know what you're chewing about."

"That's all right, Dunk. I don't reckon it makes any difference what you think about it. We've got you hard and fast, and you're done for. I reckon, too, that the captain will be glad to see you. He'll have a warm welcome for you, you bet. They certainly have you tied up for keeps," laughed the lieutenant, bending over to examine the prisoner's bonds. "They certainly have. Come on, let's finish that bacon," added the Ranger straightening up.

The party took its way back to the campfire, Stacy disgustedly throwing his gun on the ground at the foot of the tree where lay the prisoner's rifle.

"Now, sir, perhaps you will explain who and what this man is? You appear to be well acquainted with him," said the professor.

"I am that. But how did you get him?"

"Master Tad there will answer that question. He and Rector made the capture."

"You two younkers caught that man?" wondered the lieutenant.

"Yes, sir," replied Tad modestly. "But I'll admit that it was a pretty tough job. He nearly got us."

"Tell me about it."

Tad did so briefly, making as little of his own achievement as possible. He related also, how the prisoner had gained possession of Professor Zepplin's revolver and of the latter's narrow escape from death.

"Boys, you've done a big thing. The captain will be interested in you," said Mr. Withem. "He's been wanting this man for a long time."

"You haven't told us who the fellow is, yet," reminded

Professor Zepplin.

"He is Dunk Tucker, sir, one of the most dangerous customers infesting the border. We have been on his trail for weeks, but he's managed to give us the slip every time. We never expected to capture him alive. We expected to have to shoot him on sight, which we probably would have done."

"Is it possible?" murmured the professor. "I did not suppose such conditions existed on the border at this late day."

"They do not, ordinarily."

"What has the man Tucker done?"

"Done? It would be easier to tell you what he hasn't done. He's committed pretty nearly every crime in the calendar and some that aren't in the almanac. He is one of a band of thieves that has been operating on the border for months. They are smugglers and thieves. They have even gone back to the old style of stock stealing. Up to date it is estimated that they have run across the border into Mexico several hundred head of stock. The ranchers are up in arms. The Rangers have been called in to put the Border Bandits out of business. This is the first one of the gang that we have captured. And, after all, we didn't capture him. That was left for a bunch of plucky young tenderfeet - two of them, to be exact.

"Furthermore, it is suspected that Dunk and some of the other bad men of his crowd are in the pay of German agents in Mexico. The Germans are trying to stir up trouble on this side of the line, and these border ruffians are ready to do anything for the sake of easy money, even at the expense of being traitors to their country. It is believed that German money is finding its way into their pockets. The hounds!" raged the Ranger.

"Surely these men have not resorted to force - committed murder or anything of that sort?" interposed the professor.

"Not that we know of, though some of them did have a pitched battle with a rancher over on the western border of the state. A few stopped bullets, but so far as we know no one was killed. I am telling you all this in confidence. There are a good many in this thing whose names we do not know."

"You can make the prisoner confess, can you not?" asked Professor Zepplin.

"Confess?" the lieutenant laughed. "You don't know these Border Bandits. No, they never confess. There will always be more or less trouble down on the Rio Grande. It is so close to Mexico, so easy to get across the border that bad men cannot resist taking advantage of it. That is why the Rangers are still in business. If it were not for the border we all should be looking for other jobs. As it is there aren't many of us left."

"How many?" asked the professor.

"Some thirty in the state, that is all. We are subject to the orders of the governor, though we're left pretty much to ourselves."

"Who is your commander?"

"Captain Billy McKay."

"That's the man Dunk named. He accused us of belonging to McKay's band of Rangers," said Rector.

"He did, eh?"

"Yes."

"I thought so. Still, he might have shot you up just the same, even if he had known you hadn't anything to do with us."

"Where is the rest of your party, Mr. Withem?" asked Tad.

"They're out on the trail," was the somewhat evasive answer. "I'll get in touch with them sometime to-night or to-morrow."

"But you will take Tucker with you, will you not?" asked Ned.

"I reckon I will," laughed the Ranger.

"Shall we take him along for you? You have no horse?" asked Tad.

"My nag isn't far from here," smiled the lieutenant. "I'll load him on like a sack of meal. He'll get a good shaking up, but it won't hurt Dunk. He's too tough to be bothered by a little thing like that. We'll land him in the calaboose in El Paso by the day after to-morrow. Where are you folks going?"

"We planned to do the Guadalupes, then go on down to

the Rio Grande," answered Professor Zepplin.

Withem reflected.

"I reckon the captain will be wanting to see you. There's a reward out for Dunk. Captain Bill is on the square. He'll 'divvy' with you fairly."

"We are not looking for any rewards," spoke up Tad quickly. "You may tell him that whatever reward is paid, belongs to the Rangers. We are glad to have served you, but remember, we did so to save our own skins."

Withem extended his hand, grasping Tad's hand within it.

"You're the right sort, young man. I wish we had you with us."

"In the Rangers?"

"Yes, of course."

"I am afraid that would not be possible," smiled the Pony Rider Boy.

"Wholly impossible," affirmed Professor Zepplin with emphasis.

"I suppose so. However, I want you to see the captain. I'll tell you what to do." The lieutenant lowered his voice. "We will be in camp to-morrow night about twenty-five miles to the southwest of here. Know where Doble's Spring is?"

"No, sir."

"You can find it. The water gushes out of the rocks pretty high up, falling in a sort of spray. You can't miss the place. You'll hear it if it's after dark when you get there."

"And, further, you'll probably see a campfire, but sing out before you come in too close. Some of our boys are rather sudden when they're interrupted at night," grinned the Ranger.

"I should call it violent," declared Stacy. "The way you poked that pistol in my face back there was a caution. You nearly scared me out of a week's growth."

No one paid any attention to Chunky's interruption.

"Will your captain be there?" asked the professor.

"I reckon he will But I can't tell for sure. McKay is a pretty busy man. You don't know where to find him. He may be here to-night. and to-morrow morning he may be sixty or seventy miles away. You can't tell about Billy McKay."

"Is there any danger of our having difficulties with any of this fellow's companions?" asked the professor apprehensively.

"I reckon not. At least there won't be after you have come up with our party. We'll see to that."

"Where are their headquarters - in these mountains?" questioned Tad.

"We don't know. That's what we're trying to find out. We have reckoned they had their hang-out here, but we haven't found it yet"

"How many are in this band of Border Bandits?" asked Butler.

"There are some that we don't know. We do know a few of them, however. For instance, there's the Mexican, Espinoso, known as the 'Yellow Kid.' Then there's Greg. Gonzales, a half-breed Mex bandit, and Willie Jones."

"Willie Jones! That's a funny name," laughed Stacy. "That doesn't sound very savage. I shouldn't be afraid of a fellow with a name like that."

"You would if you knew him. Willie is a dude. He dresses like a city fellow with all the frills he can pile on, and he has the manners of a city chap too. But you look out for Willie. There isn't a colder blooded man in the state than Willie Jones. He's quick as lightning on the gun and can hit a bull's-eye with his own eyes shut."

"If he is any worse than our prisoner over there, I don't think I care to make his acquaintance," replied Butler with a laugh.

"He is, young man. You'd know Dunk to be a bad man the first time you saw him. You wouldn't think it of Willie and by the time you get him sized up, it's too late to do you any good. I hope you don't meet with Willie and try to land him. If you do you'll be carried out on a litter, reduced to a pulp."

"Br - r - r - r!" shivered Chunky.

"Where - where is this bad man supposed to hide himself?" asked the professor.

"I wish I knew," sighed the Ranger. "It would be worth a cold thousand dollars to me and perhaps some more. There's a price on Willie's head. But what's the use speculating about it? We'll get him some day, but he'll be a dead one when we do. I'd a sight rather capture him alive."

The boys listened to all this with deep interest. They had never come in contact with such cold-blooded discussion over human lives. They began to understand something of the things they had read concerning conditions in the Lone Star State in the early days when men's passions ran riot; when practically the only law of the land was the law of the gun. Now, conditions had changed. It was only in certain localities that lawlessness reigned in Texas, but these were bad spots, as evidenced by the presence of the Rangers, that intrepid body of men that for thirty years had been the terror of evildoers. The Rangers were pitted against a worthy foe in this instance, though it was a certainty that in time the Rangers would get their men, either dead or alive.

"And now I reckon I'll be going," decided the lieutenant, after having partaken heartily of the appetizing meal. "I'll be expecting you at the Spring when we get there to-morrow."

"Thank you; we will endeavor to be there. It will be a pleasure to meet your commander. We may get some useful advice from him."

"We'll bring up your horse if you will tell us where he is," offered Tad.

"Thanks, pard. He's on the other side of the creek about fifteen rods from here."

Accompanied by Ned, Tad hurried down, but found some difficulty in locating the horse, so carefully had the animal been secreted. Withem smiled when he saw them coming back.

"I guess you boys are all right," he nodded.

They helped him load the prisoner over the horse's back, after which, giving each of the party a cordial shake of the hand, Lieutenant Withem rode away. They observed that his rifle was resting across the body of the prisoner, as if the lieutenant were looking for trouble. The trouble came sooner than they expected. The Ranger had been gone less than twenty minutes when a volley of rifle shots crashed out.

"He's attacked!" cried Tad.

"Quick! Put out the fire!" shouted the professor.

"Don't wait for the fire. We must go to his assistance!" answered Tad, snatching up his rifle and making a bolt for his pony. "Come on, boys, we've got something to do this time."

"Stop!" commanded the professor.

"What, sit here while a band of bandits are perhaps murdering Lieutenant Withem? I can't do that. You stay here, Professor. We will take care of ourselves.

Don't worry about us. Chunky, you'd better stay here with the professor. You haven't got sand enough to -- "

"What, me stay here?" shouted the fat boy, starting for his own mount. "I guess you don't know what kind of a man I am. Come on, fellows. Whoop!"

Stacy leaped into his saddle. Ned Rector and Walter Perkins already had taken to their saddles. The professor saw that it was useless to try to stop the boys. He groaned aloud. But Professor Zepplin was very active for his years. Ere the enthusiastic Pony Riders had started to gallop away the professor had made a flying leap into his saddle and a few seconds later was pounding down the canyon, along the West Fork, in the wake of the racing Pony Rider Boys.

"There they are!" cried Tad, as bursting out on the plain they saw vicious flashes of light, accompanied by the crashing of guns.

CHAPTER IX

SHOWING GOOD GENERALSHIP

Rifles had been jerked from saddle boots as the boys swung to the left, sweeping down over the plain. Tad assumed the leadership of the party, as he usually did in emergencies.

"All hold your fire until I give the word. Keep your heads. Don't get excited!" wanted the lad.

"That is good judgment. But try to keep out of the fire," shouted the professor.

Ned Rector laughed.

"We might better have stayed at the camp if that is all we are going to do," he answered.

Tad saw that several men were riding around in a circle shooting at a fleeing horseman whose rifle spoke often and spitefully. The lad knew that the solitary horseman was the Ranger lieutenant.

"The cowards - to attack one man that way!" gritted the boy. "Now, fellows," he called, slacking up slightly, "I want you, when I say go, to yell like mad. Whoop it up for all you're worth. Then when I say fire, every man shake out his rifle, but shoot high. We don't want to hit anybody unless we have to. We'll make those fellows think the whole troop of Rangers is turned loose on them. Understand?"

"Good! Excellent head work, Tad. I'm proud of you. But I do hope none of you gets hit."

"If you are afraid, drop back to the rear, Professor," suggested Stacy, whereat chuckles were heard from the others.

The bandits had not discovered the advancing horsemen in the darkness, though had they been less interested in seeking to kill Lieutenant Withem they might have observed the little band that was now sweeping down on them.

"Now! Whoop it up, fellows!" Tad raised his voice to an exultant shout.

Chunky's piercing voice punctured the atmosphere in a blood-curdling shout, a wild warwhoop.

"Yip! Yip! Hiyi! Hiyi! Kyaw! Kyeeaw! Yip! Yip!"

Despite the seriousness of the situation and the real desperateness of their position the Pony Rider Boys laughed so that they were unable to yell for a full minute. Then they let go their voices, to which the professor added his own. But his voice was almost wholly lost in the blood-curdling shouts of his young charges.

"Ready - Chunky, aim at the moon or you'll be puncturing some of us. Now fire!"

A volley of shots followed Tad's command. Five rifles crashed out, but their leaden missiles went high, followed by another series of wild yells, whoops and scattering shots.

About this time the Border Bandits discovered the oncoming party of horsemen. All at once they turned their rifles on the Pony Rider Boys. At the first shot in the direction of the boys Tad turned in his saddle.

"Lie low!" he yelled. "Keep whooping and keep shooting. Look out that you don't hit any one. Ride straight at them. They'll give ground."

"I hope to goodness they do," shouted Ned Rector.

"If they don't it's me for the tall timber," cried Stacy, who had overheard Rector's remark.

The bullets sang so close to the boys that the lads could hear them plainly. Had the light been more certain some of them must have been hit, for those men out there knew how to handle rifles much better than did any of the Pony Rider Boys.

With wild whoops and yells, keeping up a continuous fusillade, the plucky band kept straight on.

"It's the Rangers!" They heard the words plainly, uttered by one of the bandits.

"Yip! Yip! Kyeeaw!" screamed the fat boy.

"Yip! Yip! Hiyi!" chorused the others.

"We've got 'em on the run!" yelled Tad, as the circling

horsemen swung out into a straight line and began racing across the plains, turning in their saddles to shoot at their assailants.

"Can you see to let them have a few shots into the ground to hurry them along?" called Butler.

"Yes, yes," yelled the boys.

"Be careful," warned the professor. Bang, bang, bang, bang! answered the rifles of the Pony Rider Boys. The horses of the bandits fairly leaped into the air. Soon after that they faded into dark, uncertain streaks on the white of the plain. Now the rifle of the solitary horseman began to speak again. Joe Withem was not afflicted with any scruples against shooting to hit. He tumbled one man out of his saddle, but the fellow's companions scooped up the wounded bandit, carrying him away with them. Withem thought he saw a man go down, but he could not be sure.

The boys swept past him some distance to the left of the Ranger, still shooting, their purpose being to keep the bandits going until the latter should have been driven so far away that they would not be back that night.

"Swing back!" commanded Tad. The boys pulled their horses down, and wheeling began trotting back. A little beyond they saw Withem galloping toward them.

"You were just in time, fellows. They had me on the hip for sure."

"I'm glad of it," called Tad, "for -"

"What's that? Who are you?" interrupted the lieutenant. Then he pulled his horse up sharply. "Well, I'll be jiggered, if it isn't you."

"That's who it is," laughed Tad. "Are you hit?"

"I stopped a couple, but it doesn't amount to anything. Just flesh wounds, that's all. And you boys put the bandits on the run, eh?" wondered the Ranger lieutenant. "That's another one I owe you. That's another one the Cap'n owes you too."

"Don't mention it."

"How did they happen to discover you?" asked the professor riding up beside the Ranger.

"That's what gets me. I don't understand it at all. They must have caught sight of me as I was riding out. They surely didn't know I had Dunk with me or they wouldn't have begun shooting at me. They'd have tried to pot the pony in the legs and get me afterwards, though I might have stood them off till daylight."

"Bad, very bad!" muttered the professor.

"I call it very good, sir. Those fellows have had a fright that will keep them going for some hours yet. They think it is the Rangers that's chasing them and they'll be hiking for cover at the rate of some miles an hour."

"You are sure you are not badly hurt?" asked the professor anxiously.

"If I never get any worse, I'll be satisfied. I'm a marked man, you know. Some day, when my gun sticks in the holster, I may get mine."

"Come back to camp with us. Surely you are not going on to-night?"

"Thank you, but I must be getting on. I've got to be at the camp by daylight."

"If you think there is danger of your being attacked, we will ride with you," said Tad.

"No, pard, I'm better off alone. I'll know enough to dodge them now."

"Speaking of danger, you don't suppose these men will come back and visit our camp, do you?" asked the professor.

"No, I don't think so. But were I in your place I think I'd put out my fire and set a guard for the rest of the night. It's always a safe thing to do. They won't touch you in the daytime; in fact, I think those fellows will be hiding. We'll set a couple of men on their trail just as soon as I get to camp; now that I know where the trail starts. They know I know, and that's what makes me think they won't let the grass grow under their feet."

"I am glad to hear you say so," answered Professor Zepplin. "I am afraid we should not have mixed up in this affair at all, though naturally I am pleased that we have been able to be of some service to you when you might have been killed."

"And some others with me," answered the Ranger grimly. "Well, so long. I'll talk with you to-morrow."

"Good night and good luck!" called the boys.

"Good night, pards," answered the Ranger heartily. Swinging his pony about he galloped away into the darkness, while the boys turned their own mounts toward their camp in the canyon. They had done a good night's work and Tad's generalship alone had won the battle for the Ranger lieutenant. But there were other equally exciting experiences ahead of them in the near future, in which the Border Bandits would play an active part.

CHAPTER X

THE PONY RIDER BOYS INITIATED

It was rather a solemn party that took its way slowly back to the Pony Rider Boys' Camp in the mountains. The boys realized that they had taken a rather active part in what might prove for them a serious affair. If, by any chance, the bandits learned who had interfered with them, it might be necessary for Professor Zepplin and his charges to make lively tracks for the border and seek other fields of adventure.

The same thought was in the minds of all except Chunky, who held his head erect, his chest swelled out. He was full of their great achievements and was telling what he would do if any of the bandits came to visit their camp.

"I think we will put you on guard to-night, seeing that you are such a brave young man," said the professor with a twinkle.

"On guard?"

"Yes."

"Yes, that's the idea. Let him take the watch," approved Rector.

"You forget that I'm a wounded man. You forget I've been shot twice to-day. Huh! Some of you children take the trick. I've got to take care of my health."

"I guess if we expect to get any sleep we had better let some one else do it," agreed Tad. "Chunky will have us out on false alarms all night long."

They were agreed upon this, and by common consent Butler was given the watch for the night. The boys slept with their rifles beside them that night.

The night passed without incident, Tad Butler keeping a vigilant watch all during the dark hours of the night. He had plenty of time to think matters over. He realized that Dunk Tucker, the prisoner, had overheard all that had been said during their talk with Withem out on the plain. Tad knew that if Dunk ever got into communication with his fellows it would go hard with the Pony Rider Boys.

Soon after daybreak, Tad awakened his fellows. He already had a brisk fire going, but before lighting it, the lad had walked down to the edge of the canyon for a survey of the plain. He saw a solitary horseman far out over the rolling plain. After some study he made up his mind that the man was going away instead of coming toward them.

Breakfast finished the party packed their belongings and started out for their long ride to join the Rangers sometime late in the day.

About noon they made camp for dinner and a rest, not taking up their journey until about four o'clock in the afternoon. Darkness overtook them, finding them still without sight or sound of the Spring where Withem said they would find the Rangers' camp. A consultation was held and it was decided to continue on until they picked up the party.

About half an hour after night had fallen, they were riding along when suddenly they were stopped by a stern command.

"Halt! Hands up! Every man of you is covered!"

"Oh, wow!" gasped Chunky. "They've got us again."

"Who are you?" demanded the voice.

"Who are you?" returned Tad boldly.

"I reckon my question gits the first answer, seeing as I've got the drop on you."

Tad all at once realized that the sound of falling water was in the air. With it came the thought that these must be the Rangers.

"We're the Pony Rider Boys," he said, speaking confidently.

"The which?"

He repeated his answer.

"Wait a minute. Send for Joe," said the man in a lower tone. "You fellows stay just as you are if you don't want some daylight let through you."

"I - I wish we did have a little daylight," stammered

Chunky, which elicited a short laugh from his companions. "Yeow!" bowled the fat boy as a figure appeared beside him and a pair of iron arms grasped his hands pulling him down, nearly unseating him. "Yeow! Let go!"

"It's all right, boys," spoke up the familiar voice of Lieutenant Withem. "I'd know this fellow in the dark as well as in the light. I'm Withem."

At the lieutenant's reassuring words the Rangers - for the boys had stumbled upon the camp of the men of Captain McKay's command - crowded forward, talking and laughing, three of them taking the horses as the party dismounted, then leading the way into the bushes and in among the rocks where the lads came upon a campfire, around which were seated five or six other Rangers.

Withem introduced the professor and his charges. There were, besides the Lieutenant, Pete Quash, "Dippy" Orell, Cad Morgan, Bucky Moore, "Polly" Perkins and several others, all of whom were introduced in turn, the Rangers solemn as owls, making low bows, sweeping the ground with their sombreros, causing Stacy to open his eyes in wonderment. Lieutenant Withem made the party feel at home at once.

"Just in time to have chuck with us. You see we have our chuck wagon here. Of course we don't carry it wherever we go. We usually have some central point where we make headquarters. But we have to keep changing these headquarters for reasons you understand."

All hands sat down to the evening meal after the men had washed up, in most instances without removing their hats. This attracted the attention of the fat boy.

"Say, do you fellows sleep in your hats as well as wash and eat in them?" he demanded.

"Do you sleep in your skin?" retorted Dippy.

"Yes, unless it has been all skinned off from me. When I was fighting Indians up in the Grand Canyon -- "

"Chop it!" commanded a Ranger. "Men have been known to meet their death for less in this country."

"Can't I say what I've got to say?" demanded the fat boy indignantly.

"Are you going to brag about yourself?" demanded Polly.

"I'm telling you, and -"

"Well, don't tell us. We don't want to have to take you out and tie you to a tree. Say, will you get wise to the dude with the red necktie?" scoffed the Ranger, pointing to Ned, who, in the place of the bandanna handkerchief, had put on a flowing tie of brilliant red, tying it about his neck, with the ends carelessly thrown over the left shoulder.

"Don't you like it?" asked Ned, flushing.

"Like it? Why, it's the hottest thing that ever crossed the Staked Plains since the Apaches came down in -"

"Why don't you look the other way then?" interjected Stacy.

"Oho! Listen to the human monstrosity - the monstrosity as wide as he is long and as fresh as he is stale. What you got to say about it, young man?" demanded Dippy, glancing at Tad Butler, who was smiling.

"I haven't said anything yet."

"But you're going to?"

"I may."

"Can we stand for any more remarks, boys?" asked Dippy.

"No, we can't stand for any more," chorused the men, the professor and the lieutenant being too busy with a discussion to pay any heed to what was going on about them.

"Then he shall be washed clean so that he may take a fresh start?"

"That's the idea!"

"Will you go peaceably or must we drag you?"

"I reckon you'd better drag me. If you're going to have fun with me you'll have to earn it. I don't propose to help you out."

"Do you hear?" demanded Dippy in a deep, hoarse voice.

"We hear."

"Then do your duty!"

Two men grabbed the Pony Rider boy up, Tad making no resistance whatever, a little to the surprise of the men who had taken hold of him. They expected the boy to resist, which would have given them still further excuse to handle him roughly. But Tad was used to dealing with the rough and ready characters of plain and mountain. He didn't care particularly what they did. The other boys were delighted that Tad was to be made the mark this time. They followed along laughing and jeering at their companion.

The Rangers fell in behind the two who were carrying Butler, in solemn procession. To look at their faces one would have thought they were performing a solemn duty. The boys wondered where it was going to end. They discovered a few minutes later. Tad was taken out where the gentle murmur of the Spring falling over the rocks could be heard when the Pony Rider Boys were not making too much noise.

"Do you withdraw the flippant words you used to a member of this august body?" demanded a deep voice.

"No!" cried Tad Butler. "Never! I'll die first!"

"Then take your punishment!"

With that they gave the boy a swing, one holding to the feet the other the shoulders of the lad. When they let go, Tad sailed several feet through the air. Quick as a cat in his movements Tad turned over before he landed, going down on all fours. He thought he was going to strike on the hard ground. Instead he landed at the bottom of a deep pool of water cold as ice it seemed to him. He went in all over. Not expecting anything of this sort the boy was not holding his breath. The result was that he got a mouthful of water. He came up choking, then pretended to go down again. Instead he crawled up to the bank, under which he hid.

A moment passed and the Rangers began to be alarmed. Dippy stepped to the edge of the pool and leaning over peered down somewhat anxiously.

Quick as a flash a pair of arms encircled his neck. Dippy plunged in head first. He did not even have time to cry out. The others, discovering that Dippy had fallen in, rushed to the edge shouting and laughing. Two of them went the way of their companion, Tad having jerked their feet from under them. Within sixty seconds from that time half of the crowd were threshing about in the cold waters of the pool, while Tad, who had crawled out, sat on the bank dripping, watching their struggles.

Stacy Brown was rolling on the ground, howling with delight. All at once he was picked up in a pair of strong arms and tossed in bodily. Stacy howled lustily. Clambering out he squared off for fight, but the only fight he got was another ducking in the pool.

"You - you - you fellows ought to be ashamed to pick on a wounded man that way. Don't you know I've been shot?"

"Shot?"

"Yes, shot."

"He's been shot," chorused the boys and the Rangers together.

"Any of the rest of you kiddies been wounded in the fracas?" demanded Folly.

"No, but you've overlooked two of us," announced Ned stepping out. "We haven't had our baths yet and I reckon we need them."

Without a word, two of the Rangers got up and threw the two remaining boys into the pool. Ned went in with a mighty splash, Walter Perkins landing on top of him, nearly taking away the breath of Rector. They had a rough and tumble scrimmage in the cold water, coming out choking, dripping and laughing.

All this made a favorable impression on the Rangers. Boys who could take rough handling such as this, without losing their tempers or even offering any objection, surely must be worth while. Then, too, there was the story about Tad and Ned having captured the desperado, Dunk Tucker, who was now well on his way to the calaboo se in El Paso.

"I reckon you kin go back and dry off now," drawled Dippy. "Anything else you cayuses reckon you want?"

"Yes, you might fetch me a piece of soap," answered Butler laughingly.

"I reckon you'll use sand, young man," answered Orell witheringly.

The Pony Rider Boys made their way back to the camp, wet but happy, the only dissatisfied one in the crowd being Stacy Brown. But their troubles for the night were not wholly over yet. Their initiation was not yet complete. The Rangers had still other plans for their visitors.

CHAPTER XI

BAG-BAITING THE 'POSSUMS

"Guess you fellows are forgetting about that 'possum hunt?" drawled Cad Morgan as the boys came noisily into camp.

"'Possum hunt?" cried Stacy, brightening at once.

"I wasn't talking to you," answered Morgan witheringly. "Don't break in when men are talking."

"Men? Where are your men? I want to go 'possum hunting, too."

"So do I," chorused Ned and Walter. Tad did not speak. He was watching the Rangers to see if they meant it. Evidently they did.

"That's so," answered Dippy. "We had plumb forgotten all about it. We better get a move on or we won't have that 'possum for breakfast. Ever go bag-baiting for 'possum?" he demanded wheeling on Tad.

"I never did."

"Neither did I," interjected Stacy crowding in between Tad and the Ranger. "I want to bag a 'possum."

"Better look sharp or the 'possum will bag you," warned Pete Quash.

"I guess I'm not afraid of any 'possum that ever climbed a tree. Haven't I killed lions and bob cats and fought Indians, and -"

"Stop it!" roared Dippy. "I'll be worse'n my name if you keep filling me up with that line of talk."

"What's bag-baiting 'possum?" asked Walter.

"What! You never heard of bag-baiting?" demanded Cad.

"I never did."

"Well, you fellows are tenderfeet!"

"May we go along and help?" asked Chunky.

"What do you say, fellows?"

"We might let them on a pinch. I suppose they've got to learn some time."

"All right, you fellows may go out and help us, but it's a job, mind you! You'll get sick of it before you've finished."

"No we won't," cried the boys.

"Well, I reckon we'd better be getting the stuff together," said Cad getting up wearily. "Though I'm afraid the roly-poly will plumb scare every 'possum out of the community."

"If they don't run at sight of you, they'll stand for anything short of a ghost," retorted Stacy sarcastically.

Cad did not reply to this fling. He merely grinned. Tad saw more in that grin than did his companions, but he held his peace. He wanted to see the fun, even if it were still further at his own expense.

Preparations for the 'possum hunt were at once begun. Two burlap sacks were procured from somewhere in the camp. These, with several candles and some stout sticks, made up the outfit for the 'possum hunt.

"Where are you fellows going?" called Withem as he saw the outfit starting away.

"Hunting 'possums," answered Dippy.

Lieutenant Withem smiled.

"I hope you bring back some for breakfast," called the professor. "I am fond of 'possum."

"You won't be of the 'possum they catch," warned the lieutenant, in a low tone.

With pistol holsters slapping against their thighs, Rangers and Pony Rider Boys strode from the camp, circling to the left after leaving the rocky pass where they had their resting place. They followed around the base of the mountains for a half mile. The ground was thickly wooded with second growth and mesquite bush.

Cad finally called a halt.

"I reckon we'll go in here," he said.

"Going to leave a bag here?" asked Polly.

"Sure. Here you, Perkins, catch bold of the bag."

"What do I do?" asked Walter.

"Wait; I'll show you."

Morgan very carefully lighted a candle and stuck it into the ground, packing the dirt about it with his knife.

"Now you hold the bag open. Don't move. Don't jump if you see a 'possum light into the bag. You see the light draws them. It hypnotizes them and they jump right into the light. That means they jump into the bag. The minute one hops in all you have to do is to close the bag, sling it over your shoulder and hike back to camp with it."

"That's easy. I could catch 'possums myself if that's all a fellow has to do," declared Stacy.

"It'll be your turn next, Fatty."

It was. After floundering through the bushes for some distance the Rangers stopped.

"Now, Fatty, it's your turn," announced Cad. "You may have to wait around here for an hour or two while we beat up the bushes and drive the 'possum in, but you won't care. You'll be glad you stayed when you get a nice fat 'possum for your breakfast."

"I'll catch him if he comes this way," replied the fat boy.

"You bet you'll catch it," chuckled Dippy.

"How long do I stay here?"

"Till you git a 'possum," answered Polly. "Mebby that'll be in two minutes and mebby not in two hours, but you've got to stand very still. If you move you'll scare the whole pack of them back into their holes."

Stacy squared himself, holding the opening of the bag close up to the burning candle.

"That's right. A little more to the left with the opening," directed Cad, who had constituted himself the master of the hunt. "Now hold it. You other two lads work around the outside. One of you go to the north, the other to the south about a quarter of a mile, then work gradually in, beating the bushes, slamming these clubs against every tree you come to big enough to hold a 'possum. In that way you'll drive them in."

"Yes, sir," answered Tad and Ned very solemnly.

"And go slow. Just take a step at a time, or some of the birds may get by you."

"A 'possum isn't a bird," corrected Stacy.

"You'll think it is after you've hunted one for an hour or two. Now git going, you beaters. Imagine you're beating the bush for lions. That will keep you from going to sleep on the job."

Chunky's eyes grew large.

"See here, you don't want to stand up straight," rebuked Morgan. "You must lean over just like this," bending himself almost double with his nose close to the ground.

For a half hour Stacy Brown maintained his position. By this time his back was aching, perspiration was running down his face and neck in rivulets. Insects of many shapes and forms, attracted by the light, were hopping about, some getting into the fat boy's eyes, nose and ears, others getting under his clothing. But still he held the bag open. No 'possums came his way. Some few thousands of insects did. A large part of these hopped into the bag. Others crawled in.

In the meantime Tad, his face wearing a grin, had walked away, but instead of beating the bush for 'possum, he headed straight for the camp. He heard the Rangers off to the left, as he emerged from the bush. The men were laughing and talking. Butler reached the camp ahead of them. When they came in they were amazed to see him stretched out comfortably in front of the campfire, taking his ease.

"I thought you were hunting 'possum," cried Polly.

"I thought you were hunting 'possum," laughed the others.

The men looked into each others' faces, then burst out laughing.

"Where's the other one?" meaning Rector, who like Tad was to drive the 'possums in.

"He's hunting 'possum," answered Tad. An hour later Ned Rector came sauntering in.

"Hullo, did you drive out any 'possum?" called Cad.

"Narry a 'poss," answered Ned carelessly. "I thought I'd leave them for you fellows. I didn't want to hog the whole game, you know."

"Are the other two holding the bags open?"

"I don't know. I suppose they are. They'll be even with you for that," answered Ned.

"By the way, Mr. Withem," said Tad strolling towards him, "I thought we were going to meet Captain McKay here."

"The captain is not here," replied the lieutenant with some reservation in his tone.

"Will he be here before we leave?"

"I can't say. Captain Billy may be here in the morning, then again he may not. If you miss him here, he will see you some other time. He wants to know you, pardner," smiled the lieutenant. "Where is the fat boy?"

"Holding the 'possum bag down in the bush," answered Tad with a grim smile.

The Rangers were pulling off their boots and one by one crawling into the single tent that did duty as a bedroom for all except the officers, who had a small tent to themselves. The boys were chuckling to themselves. They thought they had a good joke on at least one of the Pony Rider Boys, and perhaps they had.

About two hours after the men had returned to camp, Walter Perkins, with an exclamation of disgust, threw down his bag.

"Let them catch their own 'possums," he said. "I don't believe there are any 'possums in this country to catch. Even if there were we never could get them in a bag this way. I'll bet they have been playing a joke on me. I'm going back to camp."

Half an hour later, Chunky, his back aching like a sore tooth, straightened up with evident effort. The fat boy began to see a light, other than that furnished by the candle.

"I guess I'm the goat," he said regarding the bag reflectively. "Yes, I am the goat all right."

Picking up the candle, Stacy peered into the bag, then he thought some more. The inside of the bag was literally alive with insects. The fat boy quickly closed the bag, twisting the mouth tight and tying it fast with a string. Then blowing out the candle, he shouldered the bag, setting off for camp as Walter had done some thirty minutes before. But Stacy failed to observe the figure of a man near by as the boy stepped out on the plain. This figure followed along behind him at a safe distance, the man chuckling to himself as he watched the boy and the bag. The mysterious stranger was the Ranger lieutenant.

Reaching the silent camp, Stacy slunk in, apparently seeking to avoid being seen. The grinning lieutenant saw the boy slip cautiously to the tent occupied by the sleeping Rangers. There the fat boy very carefully deposited his 'possum bag, first having opened the mouth of it, after which he slipped away to his own tent and crawled into bed. But Stacy did not go to sleep at once. He lay there listening, gazing up at the roof of the tent through which he could make out the faint light of the sky.

Some twenty minutes elapsed when the boy sat up, thinking he had heard a sound from the other tent. This became a certainty just a few minutes later when a great uproar arose in the tent of the Rangers. Loud voices were heard, threats and shouts. The hundred and fifty-eight varieties of bugs that the fat boy had brought in in his 'possum bag, were getting in their deadly work on the persons of the Rangers. Chunky had turned the tables on his tormentors most beautifully.

CHAPTER XII

INSECTS WIN THE BATTLE

The Rangers, slapping, scratching and fighting against the armies of insects that were crawling over them, had finally got out of bed and gone out of doors to sleep. But there was no rest there either. Their bodies were covered with ants and fleas, all with well-developed biters - and they bit!

At first the Rangers did not realize the trick that had been played upon them. One who went back to the tent for his hat discovered the burlap sack that had been used in the 'possum hunt. He brought it out, holding it up before his companions. The Rangers eyed the bag, then gazed at each other solemnly.

"Stung!" groaned Dippy.

"Bitten, you mean," answered Cad Morgan.

"Which one played that low-down trick on us?" demanded Pete Quash angrily.

"I reckon it was Fatty," said Polly. "He's the one that would have thought of a thing like that. I reckon there must have been a million of those bugs crawling over me."

"I'll tell you what, fellows. Let's get Fatty out and tie the sack over his head. We'll give him a dose of his own medicine," proposed Dippy. "We can't stand for anything of this sort."

"Look here, boys," spoke up Cad. "Are you welchers? Can't you take your medicine without squealing?"

"What do you meant" demanded Polly.

"I mean that we fellows put up a job on the kids. The fat baby turned the joke on us, and right smart at that. We're It. We're full of bugs - the worst biters anywhere between the Rio Grande and the northern border. Are we going to squeal? I reckon we aren't. We're going to stand here and let the biters do their worst. I'm mighty near eaten alive, but I'm taking my medicine and I reckon I'll be taking a lot more of the same dose before morning."

"Wal," drawled Polly, "I reckon you're right at that, Cad. But I'd like to wring that little cayuse's neck just for luck."

The "little cayuse" referred to was sleeping sweetly in his tent, untroubled by the distress of the Rangers.

All that night the Rangers walked up and down, slapping their thighs, scratching their legs, for the older the night grew the harder did those fleas seem to take hold.

"I reckon their bills will be so dull by morning, after drilling our tough hides all night, that we won't feel them at all," observed Polly.

A low growl from Dippy Orell was the only reply to the remark. Now and then a man would throw himself down hoping to get a brief nap, but a few moments later he would be up stamping and scratching and growling deeply, threatening vengeance on the boy who had played the trick on them.

Next morning, Stacy Brown, for reasons best known to himself, got up ahead of the others of his party. Stacy took his time in dressing, then strolled out.

"Hullo, I guess the crowd is sleeping late this morning," he muttered. Then he halted. His eyes rested on the 'possum sack that he had left in the tent of the Rangers the night before. A broad grin spread over his face.

"I guess they won't be playing monkeyshines on Stacy Brown right away. I wonder if they got bitten much? I'm all swelled up where the insects made a meal on my skin. Hullo! Hi, fellows!"

Tad Butler and Ned Rector appeared at the door of their tent almost at once.

"Can't you let a fellow sleep?" demanded Ned. "What's the row about? Got a 'possum for breakfast?"

"No, but I've got something else for you."

"What's that?" questioned Butler.

"A surprise."

"What kind of a surprise?"

"Just a surprise surprise, that's all. What do you think?"

"Too early to think. I'm going back to bed," growled Rector. "And don't you dare wake me up again."

Tad stepped out.

"The crowd has given us the slip," announced Stacy.

"What -- why they've gone!" exclaimed Tad.

"Yes, they've gone. Gone where there aren't any Pony Rider Boys to make life miserable for them."

Tad was mystified. The Ranger company had disappeared utterly. They had slipped away silently and mysteriously. Even the chuck wagon had disappeared.

"Why, what can it mean?" marveled Tad Butter.

"You may search me. I don't know."

"Hey, Ned!"

"Well, what is it?" growled Rector appearing at the tent opening again.

"They've gone and left us and without even saying good-bye," called Tad. "Shake out the others."

The professor and Walter, having been awakened by the talking, now appeared. They were quickly informed that the Rangers had left, at which they wondered not a little.

"I guess they got tired of our company. I'm going to

start breakfast," declared Butler.

"This is most remarkable," bristled the professor. "I should have thought they would have left some word."

"How about that 'possum, Chunky?" jeered Rector.

"You better ask the Rangers. They'll tell you about that," answered the fat boy with a grin. "There's the sack in which I fetched the animals back to camp."

"What, did you catch any?" demanded the professor.

"Oh, I got some game, all right. I'm the champion hunter, I am. Say, I wish I could cook like you," said Chunky gazing admiringly at Tad, who was confidently making some biscuit for breakfast. "I never could cook unless I had everything all down in writing before me. How do you do it?"

"Oh, he cooks by ear," scoffed Ned. "That's why there's so many discords in our digestive apparatus."

The Pony Rider Boys groaned dismally.

CHAPTER XIII

AN INQUISITIVE VISITOR

Breakfast the plans for the day were discussed. The professor was for remaining in camp, hoping that the Rangers might return later in the day. Tad did not believe this would be the case. He reasoned that the men had been summoned some time during the night to go on a hike, and that they might not return at all; therefore the Pony Rider Boys would be losing time, whereas they might be exploring the Guadalupe range, which stretched away for a hundred miles.

"Still, I can't understand this mysterious departure of our friends, the Rangers," persisted Professor Zepplin.

"Perhaps it was the bugs," suggested Stacy wisely.

"The bugs?" questioned the professor.

Chunky nodded. Tad eyed the fat boy suspiciously.

"Look here, what have you got up your sleeve, Stacy?" he demanded.

"Nothing, I hope. But some of the fellows did."

"Did what?" cut in Rector.

"Did have."

"Did have what?" urged Walter. "A fellow has to have a map to follow you."

"Did have something up their sleeves."

"What was it you think they had up their sleeves?" asked Tad, eyeing the fat boy with growing suspicion.

"Oh, I don't know. Maybe it was insects."

"Stacy!" rebuked the professor sternly. Tad recalled that he had discovered thousands of insects crawling over the burlap sack when he came out in the morning. The lad's mind began to unravel the mystery. He thought he understood Chunky's references now, but Tad only smiled. He made no effort to explain, but instead, changed the subject.

"Do we start, or do we remain here, Professor?" he asked.

"It shall be as you boys wish. All in favor of going on will say 'aye.'"

"Aye!" howled the Pony Rider Boys, a shout that caused the browsing ponies to look up in mild surprise.

"Then we move. I will say, however, that I don't exactly approve of the situation."

"What situation, Professor?" questioned Butler.

"There are too many rough men in these parts. I had no idea we were going to meet with any such condition of affairs in this enlightened state."

"That's nothing. We have had some experience. Experience is what we are looking for."

"But the Rangers were not," asserted Stacy thickly, his mouth full of biscuit. "They got it, though."

"I feel sorry for you," said Tad leaning over to Stacy.

"Sorry for what?"

"For what you'll catch when they get hold of you again."

"They'd better not. I've got something up my sleeve, or I will have, I mean. They'd better keep away from me."

"Come, fellows, are you going to strike camp while I clear away the breakfast things?" called Tad.

"Let Chunky do it. He hasn't done a thing this morning," cried Ned.

"Yes, I have, too."

"What have you done?"

"I've done two things this morning."

"That's news," grinned Walter.

"Yes, name them. We don't want to do you an injustice, you know," urged Rector sarcastically.

"I made a discovery - I discovered that we had been

basely deserted."

"Well, that's only one thing. You said you had done two things," persisted Ned.

"Then I ate my breakfast. That's two things."

The boys groaned.

"He ate his breakfast. Most remarkable," scoffed Rector, imitating the professor's voice and manner, whereat the professor himself grinned broadly.

Tad, giving up expecting the others to do anything, was rapidly gathering their equipment together. The tent came down. He divided it into sections, placing the sections in piles preparatory to forming them into bundles to be packed on the ponies.

"Have you the map, Professor?" he called.

"In my saddle bag."

"I want to study it a minute before we start. We don't know anything about the trails here and we have no guide to direct us. We've got to make our way the best we can."

"We can't get lost," chimed in Chunky.

"Why can't we get lost?" snapped Ned turning on the fat boy.

"Because we don't know where we are anyway."

"Horse sense," laughed Tad.

"Fat-boy drivel," jeered Ned.

"Come, come, young men. You are not making much headway."

Stacy dragged his pack by the rope, over to his pony, instead of carrying the bundle as he should have done, Professor Zepplin observing the boy with disapproving gaze.

"Is that the way you have been taught to pack your pony, sir?"

"No. I've never been taught. What I know I've had to pick up. Nobody ever tries to teach me anything."

Scolding, joking, having all manner of sport with one another, the Pony Rider Boys finally completed their tasks. The ponies were loaded, the pack pony was piled high so that its head and legs were about the only parts of its anatomy visible, and the boys climbed into their saddles, Tad first having given the trail map a brief scrutiny.

They started off up the canyon. For a little way the trail appeared to be no trail at all. The ponies threshed through the bushes, the sharp limbs smiting the riders in the faces, making disagreeable traveling. But the young men were used to this sort of thing. They did not appear to mind it at all.

Reaching a higher altitude they found the trail to be fairly good. From there they got a good view of the yellow plains below, that stretch away many miles to the northward. To the southwest, peaks that they judged must be all of four or five thousand feet high, towered blue and hazy in the yellow light. Birds were singing, the air was soft and balmy and a gentle breeze stirred the foliage about them lazily.

"This is what I call fine," cried Tad.

"Good place for a nap," agreed Chunky.

"Are you in need of sleep?" asked the professor.

"I'm in a trance, sir."

"You always are," laughed Tad Butler. "I think we had better take a rest here. The animals are tired after the climb. Suppose we lie off for an hour?"

The boys were all agreed on this, so the pack pony was unloaded. It now being near midday it was decided to wait for dinner before pressing on. A meal was a "dab" down there and the boys had fallen naturally into the vernacular of the men of the plains.

It was Ned's turn to cook the "dab," a task that never appealed to him. Chunky at such times was always on hand while Ned was getting the meal, that he might offer suggestions and make uncomplimentary observations. Rector's method of making coffee came in for considerable criticism. He never could be induced to make coffee after the more approved methods. Ned's way was to put a pint of coffee beans in a two-quart coffee pot and boil for half an hour. He made it the same way on this occasion.

"That stuff would eat a hole through a piece of sheet iron if given half a chance," declared Stacy.

"Don't worry. It won't hurt you," retorted Ned. "Your stomach is tough enough to withstand anything."

"I guess it is or I'd have been dead long ago eating your dab," flung back Stacy.

They had to wait quite a time for the coffee, but at last the call to dinner was sounded in the usual way, the long-drawn cry of, "Come and get it!"

They had just sat down when they were startled by a voice calling from somewhere off in the bushes to the northward of them.

"Hoo-ee!"

The boys started up, thinking that perhaps some of the Rangers had returned. Instead of the Rangers a stranger rode in on a wiry little pony. He doffed his sombrero gracefully and sat regarding them smilingly.

"Howdy, pardners," greeted the newcomer. "Got a smack for a hungry man?"

"Certainly, certainly. Come right over, my friend," answered the professor cordially.

Ned stepped forward politely to take the stranger's horse.

"Never mind, lad. I'll look after the cayuse. He isn't over-fond of strangers. You're all strangers down here, eh?"

"Yes, yes. We are," admitted the professor. "You are just in time.

We are ready for dinner and there's plenty to go round."

"I'll promise not to eat you out of house and home," laughed the stranger. Without taking off his broad-brimmed Mexican sombrero he threw himself down by the piece of canvas on which the dinner had been laid, helping himself to a slice of bacon which he ate from his fingers in a most democratic fashion. "My name's Conway. Bill Conway. What's yours?"

Professor Zepplin introduced himself and the boys, which Conway acknowledged by polite bows. The man was easy in manner, and his smiling face led the boys to warm to him at once - all save Tad Butler, who, without appearing to do so, was observing the visitor keenly.

The man was slight, almost boyish in figure. His hair was dark, as were his eyes, the latter having a trick of growing suddenly darker than their natural color, seeming to sink further back in his head under some sudden stress of emotion. The brown fingers were slender and nervous in their movements.

"I'll bet he would be quick on the trigger," was Tad's mental conclusion.

"Are you from these parts?" asked the professor by way of starting the conversation.

"El Paso, when I'm at home. And you?"

"From the north."

"Down here for your health?"

"Partly. Mostly for an outing."

"Just so. I reckon I've heard something about you."

"Maybe it was I whom you heard about," suggested Chunky.

"Can't say as I have," answered Conway, directing a quick glance at the fat boy.

"You don't know what you've missed," answered Stacy solemnly, helping himself to five slices of bacon.

"You didn't happen to meet with any of the Rangers this morning, did you?" questioned Professor Zepplin.

It was the professor's turn to get a sharp look now.

"Rangers? No. Why do you ask?"

"Because we were looking for some of them."

"What for?"

"We wanted to see them about a little matter," hastily interposed Tad Butler.

"What matter?"

There was no stopping the professor.

"Why, we camped with a body of them last night. With Lieutenant Withem, a most affable gentleman. They ran away and left us early this morning. However, I suppose they had good reasons."

"Joe Withem, eh?"

"Yes, that was the man."

"How many Rangers did behave with him?"

"Twelve, wasn't it, boys?"

"Something like that," replied Tad, observing their visitor narrowly. "However, Professor, I hardly think we should speak of them. You see they were on some secret mission and -"

"It's all right, young man. You are safe in confiding in me. In fact, I am going to confide a little secret to you to show you that you have made no mistake."

"We shall preserve your secret, sir," answered the professor with great dignity.

"I thought you would. Lean closer and I'll tell you," almost whispered the visitor.

CHAPTER XIV

WHEN THE AIR GREW CHILL

"I'm a Ranger, too," confided the visitor.

"What, you a Ranger?" exclaimed the professor.

"Of Captain McKay's band?"

"You've hit it, pard."

"Well, well, this is indeed a pleasure. We have not had the honor of meeting Captain McKay as yet, but we hope to do so, ere long. He had promised to meet us last night, but I understand was called away on some business pertaining to his calling."

"You would like to meet Captain McKay?"

"Indeed I should. I understand he is a most remarkable man, that he has performed many deeds of valor."

"Pray stop!" laughed Conway. "You actually make me blush."

The outfit gazed at the visitor inquiringly.

"Now that you have said so much I am going to

confide another little secret to you. I'm McKay."

"What? Not Captain McKay, the leader of the Rangers?"

"The same."

Professor Zepplin thrust a brown hand across the table, grasping the hand of their visitor.

"Well, this is indeed a surprise. I can't begin to tell you how glad we are to see you," answered the professor with enthusiasm.

"Same to you, pardner," grinned the captain. "You see I didn't want to open up too freely until I was sure to whom I was talking. Of course if you and Withem are cahoots, it's all right."

"It certainly is all right. We had the pleasure of being of some service to Lieutenant -"

"Ouch!" howled Stacy. Tad had tipped the pot of hot coffee into the fat boy's lap, and for a few moments confusion reigned.

"Don't talk too much," whispered Butler leaning over to brush away some drops that had fallen on the professor's shirt.

"Eh? Eh? What's that?"

Tad was embarrassed. He began speaking of something else. Professor Zepplin did not repeat his question.

"I understand my men picked up a fellow named Dunk Tucker a night ago?" asked the captain.

"Yes, yes, indeed. Mr. Butler there is the one who is really responsible for the capture of Tucker, however."

"You don't say!" wondered the visitor.

"Exactly. Tad, will you tell the captain how you came to capture the man Tucker?"

"If you will pardon me, I would rather not."

"He's too modest. I'll tell you about it," chimed in Stacy Brown. Stacy, once wound up, would continue to operate until he had run down. He told the whole story from beginning to end, including the fact that he himself had been wounded twice, ere he stopped.

"Fine, fine!" The captain leaned back and laughed uproariously. "You are a funny boy. I wish I had you with me. I could teach you a lot about dodging bullets."

"I'm a pretty good dodger already or I shouldn't be here at this minute," answered the fat boy pompously.

"Where did they take the prisoner? Are you informed as to that?" asked the captain.

"They took him to El Paso, I believe," replied Professor Zepplin. "I thought you were aware of what had been done."

"I got wind of something of the sort. You see I have been away in another part of the state on a secret mission for the Governor."

"Exactly."

"Did my men say where they were going before they left you this morning?"

"No. As I have said, they left most mysteriously."

"Which direction did they take?"

"We do not know that either. They disappeared utterly."

"Just like Withem," nodded the guest, smiling. "But I'll pick him up some time to-night. I suppose they are on the track of some of the fellows who have been raising trouble around these parts of late."

"Yes, that's what the lieutenant said. They are after what they call the Border Gang. But I have no need to tell you about it. You surely are familiar with the subject."

"I reckon I know all about it, Professor. Was it some of my men who shot up the bandits the other night and -"

"No, that was us fellows," interjected Stacy suddenly. "We did give them the run. And they thought it was the Rangers too. Oh, that was a good joke. I nearly laugh myself sick every time I think about that funny scrape. We bluffed them and they ran away."

For the briefest part of a second the eyes of the visitor darkened. They grew almost filmy, then the old sparkle came into them and a grim smile appeared on the face of their owner.

"You sure are a fine crop of youngsters. You probably will be claiming the reward for the capture of Tucker, eh?"

"Not at all, not at all," protested Professor Zepplin. "My young men are not looking for rewards. It is reward enough that they were able to serve the authorities in the capture of a very bad man. We shall do whatever we can in our small way to help the Rangers round up the rest of this disreputable gang."

"Of course, of course," answered the captain reflectively.

Tad had taken no part in the conversation. He did not like this freedom of speech on the part of the professor. What they had learned were better kept to themselves according to Tad Butler's reasoning. Then again there was a faint suspicion in the mind of the Pony Rider Boy, that he could not clearly explain to himself. What did strike him as peculiar was that so much of the Rangers' movements should be unknown to their commanding officer. McKay had ever since coming into their camp been seeking information. Still, as he had said, he had been away. Tad knew that the Rangers took long rides, sometimes hundreds of miles, using relays of horses and making almost as good time as they could have done going by trains.

The lad decided that he was unduly suspicious. Suddenly, as McKay was talking, a shot sounded somewhere off on the plains. The Ranger sprang to his feet, his eyes darkened.

"Is - is something wrong?" stammered the professor.

"There may be. I must investigate. You will say nothing about having met me," commanded the stranger sternly.

"Certainly not, certainly not."

"I will bid you good day. I'll see you again when I may have something more to say."

With that McKay ran to his pony, and leaping into the saddle tore through the brush at a perilous pace. Tad observed what the others failed to see. He noted that the Ranger had returned in the direction from which he had come, rather than riding off toward the direction from which the shot had sounded. This struck Tad as a peculiar thing for a Texas Ranger to do.

"That's queer," muttered Butler.

"What is queer, Tad?" questioned the professor.

"The way he went."

"His leave taking was rather abrupt. But we know that is a way these Rangers have. Besides he thought there was trouble in the air," guessed the professor.

"Yes, but then why did he run away from it?" urged Butler.

"That's so, he did go the wrong way," wondered Ned.

"Maybe he's going to take a roundabout course," suggested Stacy.

"Exactly. You do think now and then, don't you?" smiled the professor. "However, it is not for us to criticize. Captain McKay knows his business perhaps much better than do we. And now, if you are ready we had better be on our way. We have lost no little time here."

The packing up was not a long job for not much of their equipment had been unloaded. The rest of the day passed uneventfully, the Pony Rider Boys continuing along the range of mountains.

About five o'clock they decided to make camp in a valley, beside a stream of clear, cold water. The place was thickly covered with brush and small trees, excepting for a small open space on which the grass grew high and green.

They pitched their tent near the stream. This done the boys began gathering dry wood for the campfire which would need a lot of it before the evening came to an end. Wood was scarce and darkness had overtaken them ere they succeeded in getting enough for their needs. In the meantime the professor had been laboring with the tent. He had finished his job quickly, rather to the surprise of the boys, who were chuckling over the mess Professor Zepplin would make of it. The professor, however, was far from helpless. He might not be suspicious of every one he met, but he was a man of brains. He knew how to get along with his young charges, as perhaps few men would have done. And he did get along, without friction, retaining the love of every one of the Pony Rider Boys. They were always ready to play pranks on the professor, yet there was not a lad of them but would have laid down his life, if necessary, for him.

He insisted on getting the supper, "just to keep my hand in," as he expressed it. No one offered strenuous objection to this, though no cook ever had a more appreciative audience. The professor's biscuits were beautiful to behold, but when the boys came to sample them they shouted.

"Too much soda, Professor," cried Tad.

"No, baking powder," corrected Ned.

"Wow! I know what you're trying to do. You're trying to blow us up!" howled Stacy. "Why don't you use dynamite in the biscuit while you are about it? I think I'll go out and browse with the ponies. It's much safer and I'll bet will taste better."

"Young man, if you don't like the cooking, you don't have to eat, you know," rebuked Professor Zepplin.

"Yes, I do, too. What, not eat, and with an appetite like mine? Why,
I'd eat my pistol holster if I couldn't get anything else. Speaking of eating that reminds me of a story -"

"Will some one please muzzle the fat boy?" begged Ned.

"You can go out and hide in the bushes while I'm telling the story," returned Chunky. "This is a nice ladylike story. It's about a fellow - a clerk who was out with a party of surveyors, running a line across the desert. The water holes had gone dry and they were choking for water when the clerk saved them and -"

"Ring the bell! Ring the bell!" shouted Ned Rector.

"Yes, you have told us that story twice to my positive knowledge," spoke up the professor.

"Of course he has," agreed Walter. "The clerk found water for them and they were saved," added Tad, laughing immoderately.

"Did he?" demanded Chunky eyeing them soulfully.

"Yes, of course he did. You ought to remember the story. You have told it often enough."

"How did he save them?"

"He had a fountain pen, of course, silly! Have you forgotten your own story?" scoffed Tad.

"He didn't have anything of the sort. This was another clerk. This one had a watch."

Stacy glanced around expectantly. Not a face was smiling. All were as solemn as owls.

"He had a watch," nodded Rector.

"He had a watch," added Tad.

"I wonder if the watch was running?" piped Walter.

"No, it was stagnant," retorted Stacy.

"Young gentlemen, for the sake of bringing a long-winded discussion to a close, I will offer myself as - as what you call a 'mark.' What had the watch to do with their thirst?" asked the professor gazing sternly at Stacy.

The boys shouted.

"Come down with the answer, Chunky."

"The watch had a spring in it," answered the fat boy solemnly.

"I think it's going to snow," observed Tad consulting the skies reflectively.

"Yes, the air is very chill," returned Ned Rector solemnly. "Shouldn't be surprised if some one perished in this outfit."

CHAPTER XV

MAKING A STARTLING DISCOVERY

Stacy Brown looked from one to the other of his companions in disgust.

"Ho, ho! ho, ho!" he exploded. "Hard luck when a fellow's company is so thick that he has to laugh at his own jokes. Ho, ho, ho! Ha, ha, ha! It is to smile, but nobody smiles. You make me tired."

"As I have already observed, I think it is going to rain," said Tad.

"Must be getting warmer, then. A minute ago you said it was going to snow. It's my private opinion that you don't know what you think. Ned doesn't know any more. The professor is the only one in the outfit who has a sense of humor. *He* knows when it's time to laugh. Ha, ha!"

Professor Zepplin was smiling broadly. Stacy's joke was just dawning upon the professor. But Tad's mind at that juncture was in another direction. The lad had raised his head in a listening attitude, his glance fixed keenly on the other side of the camp ground.

"Did you see something?" whispered Walter.

Tad shook his head.

"You heard something?"

"Never mind. Go on with the fun. Get Chunky to tell you when it is time to laugh."

About this time Stacy got up, still chuckling to himself, and started for a cup of water.

"Time to laugh. Ha, ha! What! Ha, ha; ho, h -"

The fat boy paused abruptly. He was down on his knees about to dip up a cupful of water when chancing to raise his eyes he saw something that caused the word to die on his lips.

A man stood just on the other side of the stream, lounging against a tree, observing the fat boy with an amused smile.

"Oh, wow!" howled the fat boy, in such a tone of alarm that the rest of the outfit sprang up and ran toward him. "Wow! Look!"

At this juncture the stranger leaped the narrow stream and was standing beside Stacy facing toward the camp when the others came up.

"I suppose I should introduce myself before matters go any further," smiled the newcomer. "I know you, but you do not know me. You are the Pony Rider Boys. I am Captain Billy McKay of the Rangers."

Stacy uttered a shrill laugh, whereat the captain shot an inquiring glance at him.

"You - you are - are Captain McKay?" stammered Professor Zepplin.

"Yes. I had hoped to see you when you camped with Lieutenant Withem -"

"Yes, we were with 'em," muttered Stacy. "And I guess we've got 'em now."

"Unfortunately I was called away on that occasion. I promised myself that I should look you up at the first opportunity. I got on your trail this afternoon and as you were going in my direction I considered this an excellent opportunity to make your acquaintance. So here I am."

"But - but -" stammered the professor.

Tad was smiling, the others gazing at the newcomer blankly.

"Well, sir, what is it? One would think you had seen a ghost," laughed the captain.

"But, sir, you are the second man who has introduced himself to us as Captain McKay of the Ranger troop, to-day."

The captain's blue eyes twinkled.

"Indeed! Then I must have a double. I should like to meet him."

"You look like the real thing," observed Stacy.

"Thank you. Then the other man did not?"

"He did not - to me," answered Tad Butler.

"How are we to know that you are the captain in person?" asked the professor suspiciously.

"I wear the badge and then here's my open countenance," answered the Ranger with another hearty laugh.

"Professor, there can be no doubt that this is Captain McKay. I should know him now from the description given to me by Lieutenant Withem. Won't you join us? We have just about finished the grub, but there is more. I'll cook something for you," proposed Tad.

"I'll join you in a cup of coffee, thank you," replied Captain McKay.

"Lucky for him that Ned didn't make the coffee for supper," muttered Stacy, but so low that the captain did not hear the remark.

Captain McKay, the real Captain McKay this time, was almost boyish in appearance. He was of about the same build as the other man who had declared himself to be the captain, but the real captain had light hair and laughing blue eyes, as opposed to the dark hair and eyes of the other man. The captain's skin was fair. It seemed not to have suffered from exposure to the sun and storm of the plains.

Tad led the way to the camp, followed by the visitor and the rest of the Pony Rider outfit.

"Most remarkable, most remarkable," muttered the

professor, taking keen sidelong glances at Captain McKay.

"You are Butler, aren't you?" called the captain.

"Yes, sir," answered Tad, glancing back.

"I knew you the instant I set eyes on you. You're a sharp young man. You discovered me before I got into your camp."

"Discovered you?" exclaimed the professor.

"Yes. He heard me. I stepped on a stick that bent down under my foot. The stick didn't snap and how that young scout ever caught the faint sound is more than I can explain."

"So, that was what you were looking at?" laughed Ned.

"Tad's got ears in the back of his head," added Stacy.

"I observe that all of you have pretty keen senses," smiled the Ranger captain. "Something smells good."

"It's the coffee that Tad's making for you," answered the fat boy solemnly. "How's the going?"

"Pretty fair. How is it with you?" returned the captain.

"So, so," answered Stacy carelessly. "You heard about my getting shot, didn't you?"

"Oh, yes, I heard all about it."

"I got wounded in the fracas, I did. I'm going to France

one of these days to fight the Huns. Then I suppose I shall get shotted up some more. You take it from me, though, I'll put some of those savages on the run before they get me," declared Chunky belligerently.

"Perhaps you will explain why your men ran away from us the other night, sir?" spoke up Walter.

"They were called away. I guess the 'possum hunt was too much for them," answered the Ranger with twinkling eyes. "You rather put it over my boys, young man," he said nodding at Stacy, whose face flushed a rosy red.

"What's that?" demanded the professor.

"Drove them out of their tent by unloading a bag of fleas on them. Ha, ha, ha! I guess you got revenge on them, young man. By the way, you're Brown, aren't you?"

"I was done brown down there in the bush that night. Mosquitoes were worse than a volley of rifle bullets."

"But - I don't understand," protested the professor.

Captain McKay laughingly explained. He told them how the Rangers had been so pestered by the fleas and other insects that Stacy had captured in the 'possum bag that the men were forced to get up and walk all the rest of the night, until a messenger had come from their commander, ordering them to go on a hurry scout some forty miles from where they were camped.

The Pony Rider Boys laughed uproariously at this. Once more they sat down with a captain, but the same thought was in the mind of each - who was the first man who had passed as Captain McKay? McKay himself did not appear to be over curious as to this. However, after the meal was finished he turned to the professor.

"Now tell me about my double," he said.

"I don't know what to tell you except that he was about your age and build, dark hair and dark eyes, a very pleasant gentleman, I should say."

"Did behave a scar on his left ear lobe?"

"I must say that I did not notice."

"Yes, he had," spoke up Tad. "It looked as if he had been shot there."

"Exactly, young man. You are very keen. I put a bullet through that ear myself, more than a year ago. I suppose you do not know who the gentleman is whom you entertained?"

"No, sir," chorused the boys.

"That, my friends, was the infamous Willie Jones, one of the most desperate characters on the Texas border."

CHAPTER XVI

JOINING OUT WITH THE RANGERS

Exclamations of amazement greeted the announcement of the Ranger captain.

"Willie Jones!" gasped the professor.

"That is the man. You see what a sharp fellow he is. I suppose he pumped you gentlemen pretty thoroughly?"

"I guess he learned all he wanted to know," replied Tad, flushing. "I don't recall much of anything that he missed."

Professor Zepplin wiped the perspiration from his forehead.

"This is most disturbing, sir. I see now that Tad was right. He counseled caution. I gave no heed to his words of warning."

"Master Tad is a very shrewd young man, Professor. I guess I shall have to take him in with us."

"Impossible! Impossible!"

"Why impossible?"

"I could not permit it."

"Let me tell you something. Willie Jones now knows all about the part you and your young men have played in capturing Dunk Tucker. He knows that it was your party that drove off his men when they were trying to get Lieutenant Withem. Do you think Willie will overlook that? Not Willie! Willie will be on your trail from now on. He will watch his opportunity and when he thinks he is safe from the Rangers he will strike -- he or his men. Then you young men will need to be resourceful, indeed, if you get off with whole skins."

"Oh, wow!" groaned Stacy. "I'll get it! I'll stop some more bullets. I'm the mark for all the lead that's flying around in these parts, I am!"

"I am of the opinion that we had better leave the border then," declared the professor.

"Oh, don't do that, don't do that," begged the boys. "We never ran away yet. Let's not do it now. We have taken care of ourselves before this and we can do so again."

"Of course I do not wish to influence you. It is for you, Professor, to do what seems best to you. If you decide to remain I think I shall be able to protect you."

"What would you suggest, sir?"

"I was about to ask if you look to spend most of your time in the mountains here?"

"That was our intention, later journeying down to the Rio Grande."

Frank Gee Patchin

Captain McKay nodded reflectively.

"That will suit my plans very well. I have come to the conclusion, from certain things that have come under my notice, that the headquarters of this band of Border Bandits is here in the Guadalupes. Search as we might we have been unable to locate their cache."

"You mean where they hide?"

"Yes, that and something else. You see their plan of operation is this. These men indulge in various forms of rascality. In the first place they steal stock when possible. This they drive over the border and exchange for Mexican goods, which they smuggle across the river and store away until such time as they are able to dispose of it. Of course there are some people higher up who are receiving and disposing of these goods. We are on their track, but we haven't sufficient evidence to convict any of them. The first thing to be done is to capture Jones and his band. When they are safely behind the bars the traffic will stop short. Perhaps when we get them all in limbo one or another of the newer ones will confess. That will make our work easier. In fact it is what we are depending upon at the present time."

"I understand. But will there not be danger in our remaining here?"

"Perhaps. There's always more or less danger, and Jones will never let up on you until either he gets you or we get him."

"I think I understand," nodded Tad. "You think we shall be able to assist you?"

"Exactly."

"Will you please explain?" begged Professor Zepplin.

"You can help us a great deal, by remaining here. It is safe to suppose that the band will devote no little effort toward getting even with you. That means that they are quite likely to hover about in your vicinity. That will narrow down our field of operations considerably. We shan't be faraway from you at any stage of the game; in fact, I think it might be well to have two or three of our men in your party all the time. Do you understand?"

"I begin to," nodded the professor.

"That will be fine," answered Tad with glowing face.

"Then we will be Rangers, too," exclaimed Walter.

"Yes, you will be Rangers, too," laughed the captain. "You are pretty good rangers already. By assisting in rounding up these men you will be serving your country, for, if we can put these Border Bandits out of business, we shall be destroying some of the Kaiser's worst trouble makers on the border."

"And get shot full of holes," added the fat boy.

"That will do you good. It will give you an appetite," jeered Rector.

"He doesn't need a tonic," spoke up Tad. "His appetite is quite enough for this outfit now. It's all we can do to keep enough supplies to keep him going. My, it's an awful thing to have such an appetite."

"Well, Professor, what do you say?"

"I am agreeable, if the boys are."

"Hurrah!" shouted the Pony Rider Boys.

"Of course, with the understanding, Captain, that you will see that we are properly protected?"

"You shall be. Of course there may be occasions when you will be going on alone. You will expect that. Generally we shall be somewhere in the vicinity. When we are all away it will mean that your enemies are also away."

"The man Tucker is safe behind the bars, is he not?"

"He was at last accounts," smiled the captain. "I am sorry Jones knows what happened to Dunk. I had hoped to keep him in ignorance of that until we had rounded up the rest of the gang. However, what's done cannot be undone."

"Where is your horse?" asked Tad.

"A little way down the creek. He's all right. Don't worry about him."

"By the way, when shall we see your men?" asked the professor.

"You should see some of them soon now. They know where I am, and a half dozen or so will be riding this way before morning, I think."

"You will remain with us to-night, of course?"

urged Tad.

"If you insist," smiled the Ranger captain.

"Certainly we insist," emphasized the professor.

"Of course we do," added Chunky. "Maybe if there are any bullets flying about you will stop them instead of my doing it. I'm tired of stopping bullets. It hurts."

"Having stopped a few in my time I think I know all about it, young man."

They could not believe that this sunny-tempered, soft-spoken young fellow was the most dreaded of all the officers of the law who hunted down the desperadoes of the border. It was also difficult to believe that Captain McKay was a marked man who had been condemned to death by these same desperate characters. Something of the resourcefulness of the man was shown to the boys in a most marked manner later in the evening.

All hands had been sitting about the fire, the boys trying to draw out Captain McKay to tell of his experiences, which the Ranger was loth to do. What experiences he did tell them were such as chiefly concerned others than himself. According to his version Captain McKay had played a most inconspicuous part in the splendid work of the Texas Rangers. Not once did he refer to the fact that he was the terror of every evil-doer in the State of Texas.

Finally it came time to turn in for the night. The captain lazily rose and stretched himself. The others were still seated, but were preparing to rise and prepare for bed when the interruption came.

A flash and a report from the bushes toward which the Ranger's back was turned caused every one of the boys to jump. Tad had his wits about him.

"Down!" he commanded.

"Oh, wow! There it goes again," moaned Stacy. "They're shooting at me again!"

Professor Zepplin had rolled into a depression in the ground, thus concealing his body from the unseen shooter. But in the meantime Captain. McKay had not been inactive. It seemed as if the bullet that had been fired at him from the bushes had barely shrieked past his ear, when the captain wheeled. His revolver - two of them - had appeared in his hands as if by magic.

Bang, bang! crashed the captain's weapons as he whirled. A yell sounded off there. Captain McKay dashed toward the spot, followed by Tad on the jump.

"Stay back!" shouted the Ranger, but Tad did not obey. He proposed to have a share in whatever trouble was before the brave Ranger captain. Chunky had taken to the bush. The others were lying flat on the ground.

As the captain ran he let go two more shots. This time there was no answering yell from the bushes. But he distinctly heard a crashing in there and drove in two more shots. He charged the bushes utterly regardless of the peril to himself, with Tad Butler close behind him. Tad had his revolver in hand, but he was cool headed enough not to indulge in any indiscriminate firing.

It was evident that either more than one man had been in the attacking party or else one who had been wounded had not been badly enough hurt to prevent his getting away. Not a sign of a human being was the Ranger able to find, though his keen eyes soon picked up the trail. He followed it a short distance, finally having reached soft ground, getting down on his knees and examining it critically.

When he looked up he found Tad standing over him.

"I thought I told you to stay back, young man?" he said sharply.

"I don't like to stay back when there's anything going on. What do you find?"

"There were two of them. Here's where they mounted their ponies. I wish I knew who they are. You see those fellows are watching."

"Watching you?"

"No. They came here to clean out the Pony Rider Boys, I reckon," laughed the Ranger. "They didn't expect to find me here. But when they saw me they couldn't let the opportunity go without taking a pot shot at me. I moved - I stretched - just at the right second, or I'd have been a dead man before now."

"The cowards!" breathed Tad, his eyes glowing angrily.

"Oh, yes, they're all of that. They shoot when the other fellow isn't looking, and they shoot to kill. But we might as well go back. I could follow them, but it hardly is worth while. They will be hidden long before we can run them down. They'll leave a blind trail pretty soon after they get far enough away to make it safe for them to stop and cover their tracks."

"But, will they not come back again?" urged Butler.

"Not to-night. They know I am on my guard now. They will put off their attack on you until some other time. Lucky I chanced to be here when they first came. I hope they don't take the alarm and keep away from you now."

Butler grinned. He hoped so too, though the others of his party might not share this hope with him, especially Professor Zepplin who was getting rather more excitement out of this journey than he had looked for.

By the time the two had returned to the campfire the others had mustered courage enough to stand up. The professor, his whiskers bristling, had crawled from the depression into which he had rolled at the first sign of trouble, and Chunky was making his way cautiously from the bushes.

"Captain McKay, how much of this sort of thing shall we have to face?" demanded the professor.

"You might have had to face a good deal more of it, had I not been here," answered the Ranger shortly.

"What do you mean?"

"That had I not been here you would have got the bullets fired at me. As I have already said to Butler, those men were after your party. When they saw me they knew they would not dare to waste a shot on any one else."

"While they were shooting you up, they knew my arsenal would get into action. They figured on killing me the first shot. But they didn't," added the captain with a mirthless grin.

"I don't like this at all," declared Professor Zepplin with a slow shake of the head.

"Neither do I," agreed Chunky. "I'd as soon be shot to death as scared to death. I'll bet my hair is turning gray already. Oh, wow!"

"All hands, turn in," commanded the Ranger briskly. "I will stand watch over the camp for the rest of the night, though you will not be disturbed."

CHAPTER XVII

FUN ON THE MOUNTAIN TRAILS

Confident in the watchfulness of Captain McKay the Pony Rider Boys slept soundly all through that night. Even Chunky forgot to talk in his sleep, thus saving himself from sundry digs in the ribs from his companions.

But when the morning came again the lads were treated to still another surprise. Captain McKay was sleeping in front of their tent door, rolled in his blanket, using one arm for a pillow. Still further out lay three other men, with one sitting up. The latter was none other than Dippy Orell, one of the Rangers. A second glance showed the boys that the other three men were also of the Ranger band.

"Hullo, Bugs," greeted Dippy upon catching sight of the fat boy.

"Hullo. You here?" demanded Stacy.

"I'm here, what's left of me."

"Bring any 'possum for breakfast?" grinned Chunky.

"No, but I've a rod in pickle for you."

"All right. Keep it in pickle for yourself. I don't like sour stuff."

"Hey, there, Bugs!" greeted another Ranger sitting up.

"My name's Brown," Stacy informed him with dignity. "When did you come in?"

"We blew in with the dawn," answered Dippy.

"And we're going to blow out with the sun," added Polly Perkins.

"Say, Kid," growled Cad Morgan, rubbing his eyes sleepily as he sat up blinking.

"His name is Bugs," interrupted Dippy.

"All right. Say, Bugs, I've got some news for you."

"I don't care about any news you've got to give out It's probably got a bullet in it somewhere. I'm sick of bullets. What I need is a little rest from chunks of lead. I'm coming down with nervous prostration as it is. Everything seems to happen around me. No matter what I do, I always get the worst of it. Why, that reminds me -"

"Is Chunky going to tell a story?" cried Ned, stepping over the sleeping captain as he came out.

"It sounds that way," laughed Tad. "Go on the Rangers are here to protect us if you tell another watch story. I reckon they'll arrest you if you try anything like that on them."

"As I was saying that reminds me of a couple of years ago when my uncle bought a lawn mower because the grass was getting so long in our front yard that the cats couldn't chew it -"

"Cats chew it?" jeered Dippy.

"Yes, before a rainstorm. They always do."

"Go on, go on. I'm pretty tough," urged Polly. "But don't drive me too far or I'll buck."

"As I was about to say -"

"You said that once before."

"I offered to run the lawn mower. Uncle thought that was fine. You see work and I never had hitched very well together. But I thought that would be some fun. So I started in mowing the yard the next morning," finished Chunky thoughtfully.

"Well, what happened?"

"Would you believe it, be - before I'd been at work half an hour, the town constable came up and arrested me for exceeding the speed limit. Now - now wasn't that hard luck?"

The Rangers gazed at each other hopelessly. No one laughed, though Walter Perkins was heard to chuckle under his breath.

"If it might be proper, I reckon I'd like to ask what being arrested for exceeding the speed limit has got to do with catching bugs in a 'possum bag?" demanded

Dippy Orell.

"Why - why - the - the constable came up in a buggy, don't you see? Ha, ha. Don't laugh. It might hurt your countenance. I'm used to laughing at my own jokes and -"

"Hee - haw, hee - haw!" wheezed Polly in imitation of a donkey. "What'd we better do with him, fellows?"

"I reckon I'd better tell him the news I was going to," answered Morgan.

"I reckon that'll take the starch out of him right smart," nodded Polly.

"Dunk Tucker has got away, Bugs."

"Em" Chunky was interested at once.

"Don't make me say it so many times. It hurts me. I said that Dunk Tucker has got away. He 'busted' out of the calaboose over at El Paso some time yesterday morning and he's on the warpath."

"G - g - g - got away?" gasped Chunky.

"Yep, and he's heading in this direction to get even with you fellows for taking him up. What d'ye think of that, Bugs?"

"Oh, help!" groaned the fat boy.

"Is this right?" questioned Tad. "Has Tucker really escaped?"

The Rangers nodded.

"That's what we're here for, to catch him up when he makes connections with his crowd again. I reckon he'll be on the trail of this outfit, first of all, before he joins out with his own outfit. He'll never rest till he puts a bunk of cold lead under the skins of the fellows who got him."

"This is where I - I get shot again," wailed Stacy. "I knew it. I knew something else would come along to spoil all my fun!"

"No use trying to sleep in this bedlam," cried Captain McKay springing to his feet. "Saddle up. I want to make the Ten-Mile cross-trail before noon. We'll find two men waiting there for orders. Professor, can you get under way at once?"

"Of course we can," answered Tad for the professor.

"Don't we get any breakfast?" cried Chunky.

"Yes, but you'll eat it cold this morning."

"Oh, pooh!"

"If you are going to be a Ranger you must be willing to take a Ranger's fare," smiled the captain.

"I haven't said I wanted to be a Ranger. I don't. I want to be a peaceful citizen."

"With four square meals a day and a whole pie thrown in," suggested Tad.

"Something like that," smiled Stacy.

The tent was already coming down. The Pony Rider Boys showed the Rangers that they were used to quick work. Twenty minutes later the boys were ready. The Rangers had watched their preparations with interest.

"Good work," said Captain McKay approvingly.

"Anybody'd think you had traveled with a one-hoss circus," grinned Dippy.

"We've got some of the animals left yet," laughed Tad.

"The Fattest Boy on Earth and -" began Polly when Chunky shied a tent stake at the head of the Ranger, thus sharply ending the discussion. A few moments later they were on their way. The boys had to ride rather fast to keep up with their escort, for the Rangers were rapid riders under all circumstances. A great deal of their success was due to their ability to cover long distances between daylight and dawn or sunrise and sunset, appearing in localities where they were not in the least expected. In this way they had been enabled to make many important captures. But the riders did not move so rapidly in this instance that they were not able to poke fun at the fat boy. Stacy was the butt of almost every joke.

To all of this Stacy Brown did not give very much heed. He was planning how he could turn the tables on the Rangers again, amusing himself with whistling, making queer noises in his throat, trying to imitate birds that he passed.

But all at once there came a sudden end to his practice.

Stacy's pony suddenly leaped to one side, planting its front feet firmly on the ground and arching its back like an angry cat at bay. Stacy did a beautiful curve in the air, landing on his shoulders on the hard ground. He had a narrow escape from breaking his neck.

The Rangers howled. They were still bowling when Stacy, getting his breath back, sat up, bunching his shoulders to get the kink out of them, and rubbing himself gingerly. The pony stood looking at its young master sheepishly.

"What's the trouble, Stacy?" cried Tad riding back.

"I - I fell off."

"I know you did. There couldn't be any mistake about that, but what caused him to throw you?"

"I - I don't know."

"That pony was frightened at something. What was it?" demanded the captain of Cad Morgan.

"I'm blest if I know, Captain. There wasn't anything that I saw."

"Take a scout around through the brush, you and Polly. There may be some one taking a parallel trail."

"Yes, there may be some German raiders hiding out there in the bush, laying for us. We ought to have some bombs. They would clean those fellows out in short order," declared Stacy.

The two men trotted from the line and disappeared

among the trees, while the fat boy got back in his saddle, somewhat more sad, but no wiser than before. But he was thinking a great deal.

"He must have got scared at some of my imitations," decided the lad. "I don't blame him."

"But which one was it? I'll see if I can do them again."

Letting his horse drop back a few rods behind the others, Chunky went over his list of accomplishments in the imitation line, trying each one cautiously, keeping a watchful eye on the ears of the pony.

All at once the eyes of the fat boy lighted up. Something struck him as funny. He laughed aloud.

"Chunky's got them again," chuckled Ned Rector.

Stacy waited until all hands were looking ahead when he tried the imitation that he believed had caused his mount to halt. His success was instantaneous. The pony leaped clear of the ground, coming down with a jolt that made the boy's head ache.

"What's the matter with that horse?" called Captain McKay.

"Guess he's feeling his oats," flung back Chunky. The boy hugged himself delightedly. What he had done was to give a trilling tongue movement accompanied by a hiss. It was a perfect imitation of the trilling hiss of the rattlesnake. When Stacy had first given the imitation he did not realize what he was doing. He had fooled his pony. The Pony Rider Boy was delighted. He tried it again with equal success, though this time he was thrown forward on the neck of his mount. This jolt nearly broke Stacy Brown in two.

"That was the blow that near killed papa," grinned the lad. "I never knew I could do that. I reckon. I'll be having some fun with this outfit. Yes, I'll try it on right now."

Stacy spurred his pony close up to the leaders. The lad's face was solemn, but it shone like an Eskimo's after a full meal of blubber. Ned Rector was next ahead of the fat boy. Chunky pretended not to see Rector. Riding close up to him, the fat boy softly gave his rattlesnake imitation.

Ned Rector made a high dive, landing head first in a thicket of mesquite brush, while his pony was left kicking and bucking on the trail. Stacy was having more trouble with his own pony.

"Whoa, there, you fool! Whoa! What's got into this beastly pinto?" howled the fat boy.

"That's what I'd like to know too," snapped the captain, wheeling his horse, giving the fat boy a quick, sharp glance.

Ned, having picked himself out of the mesquite bush, was limping back.

"You hit him, Stacy Brown!" shouted Rector.

"I never touched him. What's the matter with you?" protested Chunky indignantly.

"No quarreling, boys," warned the professor.

"Well, he doesn't want to be poking my pony!"

"Well, he doesn't want to be accusing me of poking his old bundle of bones."

"Pretty lively critter for a bundle of bones, I should say," answered the captain grimly.

"Nobody trailing," announced the scouts returning a few minutes later. The captain may have had a suspicion, but if so he kept it to himself, making no reply to the report of his two scouts.

For reasons best known to himself Stacy did not give his rattlesnake imitation again. But every little while a broad grin would grow on his countenance, which the fat boy would suppress as quickly as possible.

"This is too good a thing to be nipped in the bud," he muttered. "No, sir, I don't give my secrets away yet awhile. Mebby I never shall."

Stacy well knew that swift punishment would be meted out to him if the others caught him at his new trick, so the fat boy kept silent, looking the picture of innocence.

CHAPTER XVIII

ONE HISS TOO MANY

The Ten-Mile cross trail was made about half past one o'clock in the afternoon. Walter Perkins entered the camp on his head, Tad Butler hanging to the mane of his bucking pony, both feet out of the stirrups, Stacy Brown making desperate efforts to quiet his own mount.

The ponies had heard the soft hiss of a rattlesnake, but the ears of Rangers and Pony Riders had failed to catch the sound. Perhaps it was the yell that the fat boy had uttered instantly after giving the imitation that had too suddenly attracted the attention of the party.

"What's the matter with those fool cayuses?" shouted Dippy Orell. "What -"

Dippy did not finish his remark. He landed on his back thoroughly shaken down. He was up with a roar, starting for the pony with blood in his eye.

"That'll do, Dippy!" commanded the leader sternly. "If you'd been riding as you should have, you never would have fallen off. Now you're off, stay off." The captain uttered a bird-call which was answered in kind. The boys understood at once that the Rangers were exchanging signals. A few moments later, a bronzed, weather-beaten Ranger rode into camp. He held a few moments' conversation with the captain, after which he rode away.

"Anything doing, Cap?" asked Morgan.

The leader shook his head.

"Something may turn our way to-night. Joe has been detained. I don't know what is keeping him. But we'll wait here till he comes in. Professor, it is possible that we may have to make a hard night ride to-night. Do you wish to go along?"

"Of course we do!" shouted the boys. "We don't want to miss a single thing."

"No, we don't want to miss a thing," agreed Chunky solemnly. "I see I've been missing a great deal lately. I don't propose to miss another thing as long as I'm out on this cruise."

"He thinks he's on a canal boat," jeered Dippy.

"Maybe if I do it's because we've got some mules to pull it," retorted Stacy.

"Ouch! But that one landed below the belt!" exclaimed Dippy.

"Our fat friend has a sharp tongue," observed Polly.

"I guess we'll have to file it. Might hurt himself on it if he happened to stumble over a root and fall," added Cad Morgan.

"Chunky, are you going to get busy and help settle this camp?" demanded Tad.

"I don't have to work. I'm a guest of the management," answered Stacy.

"The management disowns you. You're out in the cold world," laughed Butler.

"All right. That's good. Then I don't have to work."

"No, he doesn't have to work," agreed the professor. "Nor does he have to eat. No work, no eat, is the motto of this outfit."

Chunky got busy at once. Captain McKay had little to say. He was very thoughtful, evidently perplexed by some word that his scout had brought him. The other men made no further effort to learn what was disturbing their chief. They knew he would tell them if he wanted them to know. At McKay's suggestion, nothing was unpacked save the stuff necessary for their meal. Of course all the packs were removed from the ponies to give the little animals a rest. The ponies apparently had ceased from their tantrums and were as docile as if they had never known what it was to buck off a rider.

Polly was getting the dinner while Tad and Ned were starting and keeping up the fire. The others occupied themselves with various duties about the camp, all save the captain who sat on a rock some little distance from the scene of operations.

Suddenly Captain McKay leaped from the rock, taking a long spring away from it, at the same time drawing a revolver and whirling. Chunky, who was passing at the time, was bowled over by the captain's sudden spring.

"Look out for the rattler!" commanded the Ranger sharply.

"Oh, wow!" howled Chunky springing back apparently in great terror. "Snake, snake!" he cried waving his arms to the others near the campfire. "Look out for the snake!"

McKay saw no snake to shoot at. Deciding that the reptile must have squirmed away, the captain, his face wearing a sheepish smile, shoved his weapons back into their holsters and strode back to the camp, where Stacy had preceded him.

There were no further indications of the presence of rattlers, and in a few moments the adventure was wholly forgotten. Shortly after dinner the captain sent his men out on a long scouting expedition, himself riding from the camp, taking Tad Butler with him. Tad was proud to be thus singled out. While they were on their ride, some twelve miles to the southward, the Ranger captain taught the northern lad many things about trailing human beings. This was all new to Tad. He listened with rapt attention, though he hoped it never might fall to his lot to have to trail men for a livelihood. The captain also told him many things about the bad men of the Texas border in the old days. Captain McKay was a lad then, but he was out with his father much of the time, the father also having been a Ranger, having been killed in a battle with a desperado whom he had been sent to capture. Captain McKay's two brothers had shared a similar fate. Now there remained only Captain Billy.

"And I expect one of them will get me one of these days," he concluded steadily.

"Why not stop then before they do get you?" questioned Tad.

"A fellow's got to die some time, hasn't he?"

"I suppose so."

"And he won't die till his time comes, will he?"

"I couldn't say as to that, sir. I guess we are not supposed to know about those things here on earth."

"No, a fellow doesn't go till his time's come," answered the Ranger with emphasis. "So what's the use in dodging? Why, if my time had come and I had quit and gone to the city to live I'd most likely be run over by a trolley car or something of that nature. I'd a sight rather die in a gun fight with a real man than to get bucked over by a hunk of wood and iron and lightning, called a trolley car. No, I'll take my medicine, as I always have and - But let's go back."

"Still it is no worse than fighting the Germans," observed Tad. "I have wondered why you have not enlisted and gone to France, you and your men? What splendid fighters you would make."

"Every man of them wants to go - I want to go. I can hardly hold myself down, Kid. Every one of us has offered his services, but the government would not hear to it. Because of the activity of the Kaiser's agents in Mexico and on the border, Uncle Sam decided that we could best serve him right here on the border, and here we are," answered the Ranger thoughtfully.

"Have you found what you came out here for?" asked Butler.

"Surely I have," smiled the captain. "Haven't you?"

"I haven't found much of anything unless you mean that a couple of horsemen crossed back there some few hours ago."

"How'd you know that?" exploded the captain.

"I saw the trail they left."

"Shake!" cried the captain leaning from his saddle. "You're the alfiredest sharp youngster I've ever come up with. Oh, it's too bad that you have to waste your talents in a city! Too bad, too bad! You ought to be out here on the plains and in the mountains where one's manhood counts for something."

"Did you come out to pick up that trail, sir?"

"That's what I came for, my boy. I reckoned those two fellows who got after us in camp last night would take this trail and head for the lower end of the mountain range. That's what they've done. This trail proves that. Of course they may get sidetracked, but that's their idea up to this point. I think we are safe in following our original plans now."

Captain Billy did not say what those plans were, nor did Tad ask him. They now turned about and started toward home at a slow jog trot, riding side by side where the trail permitted and in single file where it did not.

On the way back the captain asked Tad many questions about himself, the members of his party and their experiences during their various journeyings into the wilder parts of their native land.

"Ever think of joining the army yourself, Tad?" questioned the Ranger.

"Have I? I am thinking of it most of the time. Oh how I wish I were old enough. I know I could give my country good services now."

"You bet you could, Kid. You would make a wonderful scout over there," declared the captain, nodding.

"Some day, if the war lasts, I shall go," asserted Tad in a low voice, tense with emotion.

Billy said he had been East to Chicago once, where he had been robbed of everything he had on except his clothes.

"Funny, isn't it? I'd like to see a fellow go through me out here in my native pastures. But back there in the city -" Billy shook his head. The subject was too great for words.

They found the camp quiet and in order. The three boys and the professor had been sleeping a good part of the afternoon, and without having put out a guard, either. The captain shook his head, glancing significantly at Tad as he heard this. In fact the two had to shout to awaken the party. Then to learn that they had been sleeping all day - well, there was nothing to be said.

"Do we move to-night, sir?" asked the professor.

"Can't tell you. Not until I hear the reports of my men, and the messenger or scout whom I looked for to meet us here at noon. Seen. anything of that rattler around these diggings, Professor?"

"No, we haven't seen any rattler."

"We don't want to see any rattler," piped Chunky. "I'd snip his head off with my pistol if I caught sight of him."

"Yes, you would!" grinned Tad.

"You'd have to learn to shoot first," scoffed Rector.

"Perhaps Captain McKay will give us some lessons in revolver shooting," suggested Tad.

"From what I hear I guess you boys are pretty handy with both rifle and pistol as it is. However, if there are any drawing or sighting tricks I can show you I'll be glad to do so."

"Thank you. If we are where it is safe we will ask you to make good that promise to-morrow," declared Tad Butler.

While they were preparing the supper that night the Rangers whom the captain had sent out on a scouting expedition rode into camp, tired and gloomy. It was a personal and keen disappointment to every man of them that some ruffian hadn't shot at him once during the ride. Not once had the Rangers' weapons been out of their holsters. Whatever their mission the men merely shook their heads in reply to a questioning glance from their commander. That was all. No words were wasted in explanations. The captain knew that his men had done their work thoroughly. No explanations were necessary. This perfect confidence and understanding between commander and men was not lost on Tad Butler. It was an object lesson that made a deep impression on him.

The men had returned with sharp edges on their appetites, but they ate in silence. Stacy had little to say at dinner. He was observing the Rangers with wide eyes, stuffing his cheeks with food and listening while the professor, Tad Butler and Captain McKay discussed a variety of subjects.

"I don't understand why Joe hasn't come in, boys," said the captain finally. "He had passed Tonka Gulch at four o'clock this afternoon. He should have arrived here a long time ago."

The men nodded.

"Perhaps he's come up with Withem," suggested Cad Morgan.

"I don't think so. The lieutenant isn't due there until some time to-morrow. He will have to finish investigating the El Paso end before he can come along and join up with us."

Tad wondered how the captain knew that his scout had reached a certain point in the mountains when none had seen him or heard from him. But there were many mysteries connected with the work of these brave men. They worked in mysterious ways that added to the awe in which they were held by those whose ways were dark.

The night was warm and soon after supper the Rangers threw themselves down on the ground wrapped in their blankets. In view of the fact that the whole party might be called out all turned in early. The men had barely closed their eyes when suddenly there sounded the menacing hiss of a rattler right among them.

"Look out!" yelled Polly, jumping up.

"What is it?" cried half a dozen voices, as their owners sprang up with drawn weapons.

"There's a rattler in camp. Get a torch, somebody!"

Tad, who had snatched an ember from the dying campfire, was poking about cautiously, the torch in one hand, a club in the other ready to dispatch the reptile on sight. The Ranger who had been on guard duty hurried in upon hearing the uproar. He said he had heard a snake just after leaving the camp. The men jeered when they saw Stacy half way up a small tree, peering down at them with scared eyes.

"Afraid of the snake, eh, Bugs?"

"No, I'm not afraid of any snake. I just thought I'd get out of your way so you could work better."

The men jeered again. Morgan stepped over and gave the tree a shake, whereat the fat boy came sliding down to the ground. The search for the reptile was a fruitless one. After a time the Rangers turned in again. They had not been rolled in their blankets more than five minutes when that same fearsome, trilling hiss smote their ears again. This time the men were mad. They declared they'd find the "pizen critter" before ever they turned in again.

"Pile on some wood. We've got to have light here," ordered the captain. "Where was he?"

"That's what we're trying to find out, Captain. It isn't any easy matter to locate a sound like that. The critter may be 'most anywhere."

"Have - have you looked in your pockets?" stammered Stacy.

"Yes, maybe he's crawled in your clothes to get warm," grinned Tad.

"Oh, close up!" growled a tired Ranger.

"I was just trying to help you," answered Chunky indignantly. "You needn't get mad about it."

"No, don't grouch," laughed the captain. "We are losing too much time as it is. Better roll in your blankets and go to sleep. The fire will drive the fellow away."

Some of the men tried to sleep standing, leaning against trees. Others took the chance and rolled in their blankets. But there was little rest in the camp that night. About the time the men had settled down, they would be awakened to their surroundings by that same trilling hiss. It was beginning to get on the nerves of the Rangers. They were getting mad. The Pony Rider Boys felt a sense of discomfort too, though none showed any nervousness. It was not the first time the young explorers had passed through such an experience. Just the same they would have preferred to be in some other locality just then.

Finally Stacy went to sleep. When he woke up with a start, he tried to recall what had been going on when he dropped off. Then he remembered. He had been indulging in his famous imitation of an angry serpent. Had any of the men been awake at the moment he might have seen the fat boy's blanket shaking as if the boy were sobbing. But Stacy Brown was not sobbing.

It was some moments before he had subdued his merriment sufficiently to hiss again. The hiss was unheard. Stacy opened his eyes as he saw the captain striding into camp. He saw McKay awaken the Rangers, then start to arouse the Pony Rider Boys. In his wonderment at the proceeding Stacy forgot to hiss again for some time.

"Saddle up," commanded the captain sharply, but in a low tone.

The camp, so silent a few moments before, was now a scene of orderly activity. Every man in it was packing his pony and in less than ten minutes after the alarm had been given the men were in their saddles. The Pony Rider Boys were full of anticipation. It looked to them as if something were going to develop that was worth while.

Starting off in single file the men dozed in their

saddles, but the Pony Rider Boys did not. The latter were too much excited for sleep. All at once that trilling hiss came again. Two dozing Rangers landed on their backs in the bush. The party was in an uproar, but as suddenly quieted by a stern word from the captain. The latter wondered at their being followed by a rattler. It was peculiar to say the least.

Stacy hissed again. Then the boy shivered, for a heavy hand was laid on his arm, closing over it until the fat boy yelled.

"Ouch! Let go of my arm!" he cried.

"Young man, I think I've got the rattler this time," said the stern voice of Captain Billy McKay, as the fat boy fairly shrank within himself.

CHAPTER XIX

SURROUNDING THE ENEMY

"What's that?" roared Dippy.

"Here's your rattler. I've been suspecting him ever since early in the evening. This young man has been imitating a rattler's hiss and I must say he did it mighty well."

"What's that? 'Bugs' been causing us all this trouble?" demanded Dippy. "Let me at him! Let me at him!"

"Here, take him, but don't make too much noise about it," grinned the Ranger captain. "And don't be too rough about it, either."

Dippy had Stacy by the collar. With a powerful hand he jerked the fat boy across his saddle and such a spanking as Stacy Brown got that night he had not had since he was considerably younger. The other Rangers clamored for a chance at him, but after Dippy had finished the captain decided that the fat boy had had enough. There was stern business on hand. Still McKay thought a lesson might not come amiss at that time, so he had permitted the little diversion.

Growling and threatening, Stacy was dropped back

Frank Gee Patchin

into his saddle.

"Remember, we haven't had our turn yet," warned Cad Morgan. "Remember, you've spoiled a few hours of sleep for us fellows."

"Yes and re - re - remember you made me stand in the mesquite bush for three hours waiting for the 'possum to jump into the bag," reminded Stacy. "I guess we are about even now. But, if you want some more trouble, I'll think some up for you. If I can't think it out alone Tad will help me."

"I don't believe you need any assistance," laughed the captain. "No more disturbance now. Gentlemen, I am going to divide up our party. The time has arrived for me to tell you my plans. I have received information from one of my scouts that some half dozen of the men we want are heading for a point yonder in the mountains. They are to rendezvous at a place about three miles from here where they are to meet others of their outfit. It is my intention to surround them. One of my men is now on their trail, following them as closely as possible. There may be some shooting. If any of you wish to stay back you may go into camp right here and we will pick you up later."

"No, no! Take us along," begged the boys. "We don't want to be left behind. How about you, Chunky?" called Tad.

"No, I don't want to be left. I - I guess I'd be afraid to stay here all alone."

The captain quickly disposed of his forces, directing Tad Butler to come with him. Upon. second thought he decided to take Stacy along also, perhaps believing that it would be safer to have the fat boy under his own eyes, as there was no telling what Chunky might otherwise do.

The party broke up, leaving the spot in twos, after having received their orders, but in each case the Pony Rider Boys were accompanied by one or more of the regulars.

In a few minutes all had left the place, except McKay, Tad and Stacy. These waited for the better part of half an hour.

"Now forward and no loud talking, boys," the captain directed, touching his pony's sides with the spurs. "Be ready to obey orders quickly. And, Brown, no more imitations on your part. This is serious business. A slip and you're likely to stop a bullet 'most any time."

The three men started away, with the captain in the lead. They traveled all of two miles when McKay called a halt.

"Butler, you will go to the right, straight ahead. Stop after you have gone about a quarter of a mile as nearly as you can judge. When you hear an owl hoot, move slowly forward. Don't use your gun, no matter what happens, unless some one shoots at you. Even then don't shoot unless you have to. But let no one get past you. We hope to get those fellows in a pocket and hold them up without any shooting. But we may have to waste some powder. Do you understand?"

"Yes, sir."

"You are not afraid?"

"I am not."

"I thought you wouldn't be."

"Where do I go?" asked Stacy apprehensively.

"You will remain with me. I'll take care of you. All right, Butler."

Tad without another word rode away. Finally after having gone what he thought was the proper distance, he halted and sat his pony silently, head bent forward listening for the signal. It came at last, sounding faint and far away. The boy smiled, shook out his reins and the pony moved forward almost as silently as the boy could have done himself. The night was dark, but Tad was able to make out objects with more or less distinctness. He used his eyes and ears to good purpose. Once Tad thought he heard a twig snap a short distance ahead of him. He halted abruptly and sat steadily for fully ten minutes. There being no further sounds he moved forward again.

It was a trying situation for a boy. Tad Butler felt the thrill of the moment, but he was unafraid. It is doubtful if Tad ever had realized a sense of fear, though he was far from being foolhardy, nor was there the faintest trace of bravado about him. He was simply a steady nerved, brave lad who would do his duty as he saw it no matter how great the obstacles or how imminent the peril.

The boy had gone forward for some thirty minutes when all at once his quick ears caught a peculiar, low whistle some distance ahead. Tad with ready resourcefulness answered the whistle, imitating it as nearly as possible. But he made a mistake. That whistle was not the right whistle.

Bang!

A flash of flame leaped toward him and he heard the "wo-o-o-o" of a bullet over his head. The boy was off his pony. Then Tad tried the tactics of an Indian. Quickly and silently tethering his pony, he fired a shot high enough so that he did not think it likely to hit any one. Skulking a few paces farther on, he fired again. Several shots were in this manner fired, and in quick succession, giving the impression that there were several men shooting.

Half a dozen answering shots were fired at him, then the lad caught the sound of hoofbeats. He knew the other man was riding away. Tad gave the hoot of an owl as best he could. Rather to his surprise the signal was answered off to the left. Tad repeated it and received the same answer. He rode forward, on the trail of the fleeing man. In a few minutes he was joined by Captain McKay and Stacy, both riding hard.

"Did you draw them out?" demanded the captain sharply, but without a trace of excitement in his tone.

"Yes." Tad explained what had occurred.

"That was one of the outposts. The others will begin to stir soon. We are too early. All the ruffians are not in yet. Well, it's too late now. The alarm has been given. There they go!"

A succession of shots followed from distant points, widely separated. McKay listened.

"Our men are shooting. It's time to close in. Stick behind me. Don't try to ride off to one side. Keep your eyes and ears open."

The ponies leaped forward. The man and the two boys were riding a dangerous pace considering the roughness of the trail, but none gave a thought to the danger. The captain's voice was raised in a long-drawn hoot, which was answered by another from some distance away. Then the firing broke out afresh. It seemed as if no one could escape that fusillade of bullets. Tad could hear the bullets screaming overhead. He sat his pony, his eyes glowing, firing rapidly into the air. Stacy Brown also sat his own pony, but he couldn't have moved a muscle to save him. The fat boy was literally "scared stiff." Stacy really was suffering, but no one, unless he had observed his eyes, would have thought him afraid.

"Close in, boys. Ride and shout!" commanded the captain.

Butler exercised his lungs. Chunky's lips moved, but no sound came from them. His pony, however, followed the others, nearly causing its stiffened rider to fall off.

Every few moments the captain would utter his owl-call, which would be answered by other similar calls pretty much all around the compass. In this way the Rangers were able to locate each other's positions, thus avoiding shooting each other.

The shots of the enemy were now scattering.

It was only occasionally that McKay was able to determine that one of the bandits had fired a gun. How he could tell the difference between the rifles of friends and foe was a mystery to young Butler. Ere long the Rangers had narrowed down their circle until they were able to see each other. For the past twenty minutes, they had been stalking cautiously. Now they paused, after having exchanged signals. Deep growls were heard on all sides.

"What does it mean?" questioned Tad.

"It means those fellows have given us the slip again," grunted the captain. "They've managed to slip through our lines somehow. Well, never mind, we'll get them one of these times. I thought we had them pocketed this time so there would be no escape."

Tad had thought so, too. He was convinced that there was more to this escape than even the Ranger captain realized. The boy did not wish to make suggestions so he kept silent. Yet he determined to make an investigation on his own hook on the following morning, provided they were anywhere in that vicinity.

There was nothing more that the Rangers could do. Their prey had eluded them, disappearing as suddenly as if through a hole in the earth. It was the first time that such a thing had occurred to Captain McKay and his failure bothered him, but he presented a smiling face when, after having withdrawn a mile or so, the men went into camp for the rest of the night, building up a campfire and putting out a heavy guard to prevent a surprise during the night.

"Don't you think the rascals have a hiding place there where they evaded us so neatly?" asked Tad, upon getting the captain's ear.

"There is no hiding place there. I know the locality well," was the terse reply.

"But surely they could not have got through your lines," objected the boy.

"Yet they did. That's all there is to it."

Not a man of the Rangers had been hit, nor was it believed that any of the enemy had been wounded. Night shooting at skulking figures in a forest is uncertain work. Tad realized a sense of thankfulness for this. He was not anxious to see bloodshed, but now that the danger was over, Chunky grew very brave. He told them all about it and how "We" had driven the bandits off. The story grew and grew with the telling until Stacy was convinced that he had fought a very brave battle.

Tad lay awake a long time that night thinking over the occurrences of the evening, pondering and seeking for a solution of what he considered was a great mystery. On the following morning the greater part of the band were off at an early hour, before the boys had risen, on a day's scout, to try to pick up the trail of the bandits. It was to be a day of excitement for some of the party and hard work for others, for many miles would be covered by the Rangers before their grilling ride came to an end.

CHAPTER XX

LEARNING SOME FANCY SHOTS

After breakfast Captain McKay took an hour's ride alone over the surrounding country. In the meantime the boys pitched a more permanent camp as it was more than likely that they would remain there for another night, since McKay did not seem to want to leave the place just yet. What he had in mind the boys did not know.

Returning from his ride the captain appeared to be in much better spirits. His was a strange make-up. None wholly understood Captain Billy. Perhaps that was one of the reasons for his success in his perilous calling.

"Well, I promised to give you boys some lessons in revolver shooting," he said, tossing the reins to Tad who had come forward to take the pony. "Who can put a hole through my sombrero?" cried the Ranger sending his broad-brimmed Mexican hat spinning up into the air.

A flash and a bang followed almost on the instant. The Pony Rider Boys howled. The shot had been fired by Professor Zepplin and he had drilled a hole right through the Ranger's sombrero.

Frank Gee Patchin

"Well, now, what do you think of that?" gasped Chunky, his eyes growing large. "I didn't think you could hit the side of a barn unless you were inside the barn."

The professor smiled grimly.

"I used to be counted the best revolver shot in my regiment when I was in the army. But I'm a little slow these days."

"Humph! I see you are," grunted Billy. "Lucky for me that you aren't quick or I wouldn't have had any hat left by this time. Anybody else want to try to put a hole through my hat?" he asked looking about.

"I was going to suggest that we throw up the professor's hat and let you take a shot at it," suggested Tad, coming up at this juncture.

"Here it goes," cried the professor sending the hat spinning away from them, with the edge of the brim almost toward them. The hat was spinning low and a very difficult mark to hit.

Tad thought the Ranger was going to take a shot at it, but instead of doing so, McKay nodded to Tad, with a merry twinkle in his eye.

Tad whipped out his revolver with a quickness that amazed the Ranger, and let go. His bullet snipped a piece from the edge of the rim. The force of the bullet turned the hat crown toward the shooter.

Bang, bang, bang! Tad bored three holes through the crown to the captain's amazement.

"There! I guess we are even with you now, Professor," laughed the boy. "That old hat of yours won't hold water next time you go to the spring."

"I thought you folks didn't know how to shoot," wondered the Ranger. "I guess I'd better take some lessons from you instead of you from me. That certainly was mighty fine gun work. Where did you learn?"

"Since we have been out. I am not much of a shot with the revolver, though. I think I can do better with the rifle."

"How about the rest of you?" questioned the captain. "Do all of you shoot like that?"

"I suppose I am about the best shot in the outfit," answered Stacy pompously. "I can hit a penny -"

"Yes, if the penny is glued to the muzzle," interrupted Ned.

"We'll see what you can do."

Stacy, after three shots, failed to hit the hat once. Walter and Ned each succeeded in placing a bullet through the professor's hat. Chunky insisted that his bullet went through one of the holes made by Tad Butler. He declared that he had never missed an easy shot like that in his life.

"Here, hit my hat," commanded Tad, tossing his sombrero into the air.

The fat boy watched the soaring hat with longing eyes.

"Shoot, shoot, why don't you?" jeered the Pony Rider Boys.

"All right if you say so."

Stacy's pistol stuck in the holster and by the time he had freed the weapon the sombrero was only some seven or eight feet from the ground.

"Yeow!" howled the fat boy letting go two bullets with a speed that they had no idea he possessed.

"It's a hit!" cried the professor.

Tad ran forward and picked up the hat.

"Well, what do you think of that?" he wondered.

"Did he hit it?" called Walter.

"Of course he did."

"Oh, pooh! That hole was in your sombrero before he shot," scoffed Ned Rector.

"You are wrong. There were no holes in the hat. Now there are two. Stacy sent two bullets through my hat instead of one."

"Hooray!" shouted the boys.

"I didn't think it of you, Brown," smiled the captain. "I take back all I have said against your character and your ability."

"Oh, don't mention it. That's nothing. I usually shoot

my hat full of holes before breakfast every morning when I'm home. Anybody else want his hat transformed into a sieve?"

"I think you have done quite enough," returned the professor. "You have done fully as well as I could have done. Ahem!"

"Really remarkable shooting for tenderfeet," declared the captain.

"Tenderfeet? Well, I like that!" grumbled Stacy. "Why, I'm a lion fighter, I am!"

"And a snake man as well," grinned the Ranger.

"Yes. I'm no tenderfoot. Did I run away when the shooting was going on last night? I guess not. I -"

"No, he was too scared to run," snorted Rector.

Stacy regarded Ned solemnly.

"Ned Rector, I don't usually acknowledge you to be right in matters like this, but I'm going to admit before the whole company that you've told the truth for once in your -"

"I always tell the truth," broke in Ned.

"-life," finished the fat boy. "I was, as our distinguished fellow - tenderfoot says, scared stiff. But if the truth were known, I'll wager that he was hiding behind a rock when that same shooting was going on."

Rector flushed a rosy red, which brought a howl from

the boys. It was plain that Chunky had touched him in a tender spot.

"Come now, you boys, if you want to try some more," called the Ranger.

"What now?" asked Tad.

"I want to see how you are on the draw - quick." The captain trimmed a piece of paper down to about the size of a silver dollar. This he pinned to a tree, then measuring off twenty paces, faced the mark, spun about on his toes, making two complete whirls and drove a bullet right into the center of the target, having drawn his revolver as he turned. It was a splendid piece of shooting.

The professor missed. He did not even hit the tree. Tad took a piece out of the edge of the target the first time. The second he placed a bullet just inside the outer edge, which McKay pronounced to be excellent shooting. That was high praise from a man like Billy McKay.

Ned did not know whether he wanted to try that shot or not. McKay explained how to draw quickly and at what point of the whirl to draw, but try as he would Rector could not hit the mark. Once he chipped a piece of bark from the tree, which brought a yell from the boys.

"The trouble with you lads is that you grip your guns too tightly. Take a light hold on the butt of your revolver. Toy with it. It's the fellow with the feather-weight touch that does the best work with the revolver. He is the man to look out for."

"That's the way I always shoot," declared Chunky pompously. "If there's one shot that I can make better than another it's that one you fellows have been trying. Why, I could pink that target with my eyes shut."

"Try it. See what you can do. Perhaps you may beat us all, who knows?" grinned McKay.

"I don't say that I can beat *you*, but I can shoot as well as these amateurs who have been trying it. I can -"

"Look here, are you going to make that shot, Chunky?" demanded Rector.

"Yes. Got any objections?" asked Chunky turning to Rector with great deliberation.

"Not the least, if you'd kindly hold your fire till I can get behind a rock or a thick tree."

"Yes, that's the place for you, I reckon. All ready, Mr. McKay?"

"It's up to you," smiled the Ranger. "Does it make any particular difference to you which way I whirl?" asked the fat boy.

"Not in the least. You may stand on your head and whirl if it will suit you better."

"For goodness' sake, do something," begged Tad. "You've taken enough time already to shoot the tree clean off the map."

"Who's doing this shooting, you or I?" asked Chunky.

Tad sat down helplessly. Stacy was not to be hurried. The more one urged him, the slower did he become.

"Look out, I'm going to shoot now. Everybody lie low!"

Stacy spun himself around like a top. He had whirled three times when the Ranger shouted to him.

"Shoot before you get so dizzy you can't see!"

Bang!

"Stop it -"

Bang!

"Stop it, you idiot!"

McKay struck the fat boy's revolver just in time to prevent getting a bullet through his own body. Over yonder the professor lay flat on the ground with a frightened look on his face, shouting at the top of his voice.

"Hold him! Hold him! He'll have us all riddled!"

"Wha - what's the matter?" demanded Stacy looking around innocently.

"Matter? See what you have done."

"Di - did I wing the professor?" questioned the fat boy innocently.

"Did you wing him!" jeered Tad Butler.

"Come here, young man. But leave that pistol behind you," commanded Professor Zepplin. "I think we will equip you with a small bow and a blunt arrow after this. Even. then I fear our eyes will be in danger. Do you see what you did?"

One of Stacy's bullets had bored a hole through the crown of the professor's sombrero. The other had plowed a neat furrow through Professor Zepplin's grizzled whiskers, close to the chin.

"Ho, ho, ho! Haw, haw, haw!" roared the fat boy with head thrown back as far as it would go without dislocating his neck.

CHAPTER XXI

A HOLE IN THE MOUNTAIN

The professor gave Stacy a shaking that the fat boy did not forget at once, the others shouting their approval. The fat boy grinned after his punishment.

"I'm a regular William Tell, eh?" he asked looking about. It was still a good joke to him. Even the professor permitted a grim smile to show itself at the base of his whiskers.

"You came near killing Professor Zepplin," answered the Ranger.

"That would have been too bad," replied Stacy almost anxiously. "I shouldn't have had anybody to tease then. Do I try that shot again?"

"You do not!" was the firm reply from McKay.

"I guess I knew what I was about when I hid behind that rock," laughed Rector.

"According to Chunky, you knew what you were about when you got behind the rock during the shooting yesterday," cut in Tad.

"Come, come, boys, if you are going to shoot any more you'd better get busy. I shall soon have to leave you. Who shoots next?" demanded the captain.

"I do," announced Stacy.

"You shoot no more in this camp, young man," insisted the professor. "It's all right for those who know how, but you endanger our lives with your irresponsible actions."

"All right, Butler, I will now throw my hat up from behind you. You will turn and shoot at it when I give the word," said the captain.

The first shot Tad missed the hat by some three or four rods. How the boys did shout and jeer at him!

"I did better than you. I trimmed the professor's whiskers," declared Chunky.

Tad nodded to McKay that he was ready for another shot.

"Don't shoot this time until you see the hat. Shoot a little under rather than over it. The natural tendency is always to overshoot, whatever one is shooting at."

Bang!

The hat in the air jumped as if it had received a sudden blow as Tad whirled and let go.

"You've graduated. Next!"

Rector missed five shots. Walter fanned the rim, then

they called a halt in the practice.

"Altogether I am well satisfied with your shooting, boys. Even Brown accomplished something," said McKay.

Stacy grinned broadly.

"I - I could hit a German, couldn't I?" he stammered.

"Yes, I think you could," laughed Billy.

"Especially if you were to turn your back to him before shooting," added Tad.

"Professor," said McKay, "I must go away for part of the day. I do not believe your party will have any difficulty. The bandits are no longer here. I should not be at all surprised if my men were to round them up, as they are on the track of the enemy at this very moment. If you want to move, you may do so, but I would suggest that you make this your camp for the night"

"I am quite well satisfied here. The boys will no doubt want to go out exploring. I am somewhat interested in the geological formation of the canyon at this point, so we shall all be well occupied during the remainder of the day. You plan to return here to-night?"

"I think so."

"We will see if we can't pick up the trail of the enemy," laughed Tad.

"Do so by all means. Who knows but that you may discover something worth while? I am sure you have an idea in your mind," answered McKay, giving Butler a shrewd glance.

"I will confess that I have, sir."

The Ranger captain did not say where he was going. But shortly after that he rode out of camp and was seen no more until late that evening. After the departure of McKay the professor cleared his throat and stroked his damaged whiskers.

"I trust you young men will try to keep out of trouble to-day. I am sorry to say that you are becoming rather too venturesome. Be good enough to keep in mind that we are in what appears to be a hostile country."

"It strikes me that Chunky is more hostile, more to be feared, than anything else about here," chuckled Tad.

"I agree with you, and for that reason I am going to place Stacy under your charge for the day, Tad."

"Oh, what a responsibility!" mocked Butler.

"I'm glad it isn't up to me," declared Ned.

"You will look after Walter."

"I don't need any looking after," protested Perkins.

"That's why he's put you in charge of Ned," scoffed Stacy.

"Shake hands. We will take a fresh start, Chunky," said Ned, extending a friendly hand.

Chunky regarded Ned suspiciously. He wondered what Rector had in mind to induce him to become so friendly all at once. As it chanced Ned felt that perhaps he had been rather too hard on the fat boy. But the fat boy had never thought of it in that light. Each was supposed to take the jokes played on him and without losing his temper. As a rule each one did, though Chunky seemed to get more than his share of such abuse. Perhaps he brought his troubles on himself.

"Well, if I am going to have charge of you, Stacy, I think I'll take you out in the woods where you can't do any damage to any one but myself. Bring your gun and we'll go shooting."

"My rifle?"

"No. Your pistol."

"That suits me. I am too delicate to tote a rifle around on my shoulder all day."

"Be back early, and do not go far away," ordered the professor.

"Shoot off a rifle if you want us before we get back," suggested Tad.

"Which way are you going?" asked Ned.

"South. Which way do you go?"

"I guess we will go west if you are going south. I want to get a good distance away if you fellows are going to shoot at a mark."

"Come on, Stacy."

The fat boy and his companion strolled off. They were going to take their ponies, but the professor had decided against this, fearing that the boys would stray too far from camp were they to ride. Being on foot he felt reasonably certain that they would not get far away, knowing how averse they were to walking, which is usually the case with those used to riding a horse. A cowboy will mount his pony if he wants to go across the street, just the same as a fire chief will get into his buggy if he goes to a fire on the same block.

Stacy and Tad engaged in a friendly conversation on the way out. Tad was giving his companion some advice. They were talking seriously and for a wonder Stacy was giving serious consideration to what Butler was saying.

They had been going along aimlessly for nearly an hour, halting now and then to sit down on a rock or a log, when Stacy paused, looking about him curiously.

"Isn't this the place where we were shot at last night?"

"Yes, this is the place, I guess," answered Tad, looking about him inquiringly. "Over yonder is where we were stationed. Let's go over and look about a little."

Stacy was willing, so they strolled over. Tad sat down, a thoughtful look on his face, taking a survey, forming a mental picture of the scene as it had appeared during the bloodless battle with the border bandits.

"According to my idea those fellows must have fallen into a hole in the ground about where that tree is down," declared Stacy wisely.

"That is my idea too," answered Tad. "I can't understand how they could have slipped by us as easily as they did."

"Maybe they didn't."

"They must have done so. There is no hole in the ground over there, as you can see for yourself. Even if there were, what good would it have done the men? Let's go over and see if we can pick up a trail of some sort."

"I'm with you. Where shall we begin?"

"You go to the left and I'll go to the right. We will meet somewhere near the fallen tree unless we get side-tracked."

The tree referred to was a huge one. It lay at the base of a great pile of rocks, from which it evidently had slipped. In falling it had carried its roots with it. These roots, massed with dirt and stone, stood up in the air all of fifteen feet. The top of the tree was a hundred feet further out. It must have been a magnificent tree when it stood towering from the top of the rocks there and no doubt was a landmark for all that part of the Guadalupe Range. The trunk at the top stood free of the ground several feet, the trunk nearer the roots resting on an almost knife-like edge of rock that had cut deeply into the trunk when the tree fell.

Stacy gazed at the tree and decided that it would make an excellent thing to climb. He stepped up on the trunk at the roots, walking out toward the top.

"Come on up. The walking's great, Tad," he cried.

"I'll be there pretty soon."

After looking about for several minutes Butler followed his companion. But Tad paused before climbing up. He eyed that towering mass of roots, dirt and stones with interest.

"See anything funny?" called Stacy.

"No, nothing particularly funny. I do see the print of a horseshoe here on the rocks where some dirt has stuck to the shoe and been left on the stone. It isn't any of our stock as nearly as I can determine. I guess it must have been some of those fellows last night. They evidently were shooting from behind the tree here."

"They weren't shooting from behind much of anything, as well as I could judge," answered the fat boy.

Tad climbed up and made his way slowly along the tree trunk. As he neared his companion, he felt the tree settle a little. This at the moment did not make any particular impression on the Pony Rider Boy. Their combined weight might cause the outer end to give a little. Then all at once a howl from Chunky caused Tad to grasp a branch to save himself.

The tree top was settling slowly.

"Look, look!" cried the fat boy.

Tad turned, amazement growing on his face. The roots of the tree had slowly risen several feet into the air, disclosing a hole in the rocks.

Chunky was so excited that he fell off before Tad could say a word. The tree settled back, closing the hole in the rocks.

CHAPTER XXII

THE CAVE OF THE BANDITS

The top of the tree sprang up with such force, when relieved of the weight of the fat boy, that Tad Butler lost his hold and was catapulted to the ground, which he struck with a force that made his bones ache.

The two Pony Rider Boys sat up rubbing themselves and looking into each others' faces.

"Well, what do you think of that?" jeered Stacy Brown.

"I think we got a fine tumble," replied Tad, grinning.

"And I think something else, too."

"Yes, we've made a discovery!"

"A great discovery," breathed Stacy tensely.

"I think so, but that remains to be seen. Who would have thought it? But get away from here! We may have disturbed some one."

The lads quickly scrambled up and, skulking into the bushes, crouched down, watching the roots of the tree, almost expecting them to rise into the air again.

Frank Gee Patchin

Nothing of the sort happened. The birds were singing in the trees, the sun was shining brightly, the heat was intense.

"I'm going to investigate," declared Tad.

"Maybe we've discovered another gold mine, or perhaps a German dugout," suggested Chunky.

"Perhaps, but not in the way you think."

"How do you mean?"

"Wait until we investigate. There may be more to this than either of us think. I wonder if we can weight that tree down so the roots will stay up in the air?"

"I saw some rocks there near the top. Perhaps we can make them stay on so the top will be held down."

"You get up on the tree again and I'll pass the rocks up to you. Place them so they won't slide off. I don't want to get crushed by them falling on me."

"Neither do I want to get thrown off again. I'm black and blue all over, right this minute."

"I think I must be by the feel of my skin. Hurry!"

Stacy ran back to the roots, once more clambering to the trunk, along which he ran clear to the outer end. Tad was ready with a heavy, flat rock which he carefully raised by main strength.

"Now, don't you dare let that drop on me or I'll be mashed flat, Stacy Brown."

"I - I won't let it d-d-rop un - unless I - I fall off."

The rock nearly got away from the fat boy. Butler leaped back out of the way, but Stacy recovered himself in time and after some effort succeeded in placing the rock in the limbs of the tree.

"Fits as if it had been here before," declared Chunky.

"Perhaps it has. We shall see. Are you ready?"

"Yep."

"Here's another."

By the time the third stone had been put in place the top of the tree began to settle. The fourth rock brought the tree down to the ground, exposing the opening in the rocks once more.

"Hurrah!"

"Keep still. Don't move till I get enough up there to equalize your weight. Then you may come down."

The remaining stones were quickly laid in place. Tad motioned for Chunky to descend. The fat boy leaped down. The tree top remained on the ground leaving a wide opening in the rocks.

"Now, Chunky, keep your nerve. You may need it."

"What are you going to do?"

"I'm going in there. I think perhaps it might be the wiser plan for you to remain out here and keep watch."

"No, sir, I guess not! I've helped discover that hole and I'm going to reap my reward by exploring the inside."

"Come along then. It is taking long chances, but I guess the tree is safe unless some one should come along and trip the stones. Then we would be in a fine fix, shouldn't we?"

"I reckon we would. We wouldn't be getting out of that hole, right smart, should we, Tad?"

"I guess not. We should be buried alive."

"Still, there may be some other opening to the place. We will take a chance. Got your matches?"

"Yes."

"Then you light a match when we get inside. I'll have my revolver ready in case there is anything in there."

Taking a final glance about, Tad moved toward the opening in the rocks with brisk step. Chunky was trotting along behind him, the fat boy full of importance over the discovery they had made. At the opening they paused, glancing apprehensively at the great roots towering above them. Were the butt of that giant tree to settle down now, it would crush them.

The boys stepped inside. They could see but a few feet ahead of them, but saw that they were in a huge crevice in the rocks, a sort of cave formed by the splitting apart of the rocks themselves, perhaps from some long past earthquake disturbance.

"Light a match, Stacy."

The fat boy did so.

"There have been horses in here," announced Tad.

"Yes, I guess there have, but there aren't any here now."

"Fortunately for us."

The air was cool, though a little damp in the cave. To this the boys gave no heed. They had more important matters on hand than observing the atmosphere of the place. The cave they found was much larger than they had had any idea of. In places the roof was all of ten feet high. But as they penetrated further in, moving cautiously, lighting the way with every step, the walls sloped toward the back, approaching nearer to the floor.

Except for the light from the matches, the boys were in darkness, so that they were not able to observe that the opening to the cave had closed. A strong breeze, swaying the upper limbs of the tree, had dislodged the stones and allowed the roots to slip quietly into place again. The boys, without knowing it, were prisoners.

"You aren't throwing your matches on the floor, are you?" demanded Tad turning sharply.

"Yes, why not?"

"Show me a light here," commanded Tad going down on his knees and gathering up all the burnt matches he could find. "That is a fine trail you are leaving. Why, were any one to come in here, he would discover instantly that strangers had been here."

"I - I never thought of that," stammered Chunky.

"We must think of everything. Our very lives may depend on our doing so."

"Wha - what do you mean, Tad?"

"Don't you understand yet?"

"I - I guess I begin to. Some - somebody's been here."

"Yes. It is my opinion that the very men Captain McKay is looking for have been here. Come, we must be quick! We are likely to be interrupted at any time, though I hardly think any of them would come here in the daytime."

The boys were obliged to stoop in order to continue their explorations further. After creeping under the low-hanging rock they found that they were able to stand erect once more. Then they discovered something else. There were bales piled on top of one another, packs securely tied lying about, guns, rugs, in fact a miscellaneous assortment of goods which the boys believed to be of great value. In one corner stood a chest securely padlocked. It was a rough chest, bound with iron bands that looked as if they might have been used on cotton bales.

"Well, we have made a discovery, Stacy Brown!" breathed Tad.

"We have," agreed the fat boy, his eyes growing large with wonder. "What do you suppose is in that chest?"

"I don't know."

"Let's open it," suggested Stacy eagerly.

Tad shook his head.

"In the first place we have no business to do anything of the sort. In the second place I don't want to stay here much longer. We had better be getting back to camp as quickly as we can. Of course we can't do anything until Captain McKay returns, but the more quickly we get away from here the better it will be for us."

"I - I'm scared. Aren't you?" stammered the fat boy apprehensively.

"No, I am not scared, but I realize that we are in danger every minute we stay here. Those men wouldn't trifle with us, were they to catch us. Do you know what they would do to us if they caught us here, Chunky?"

"Nu - nu - no."

"They would fill us full of lead, that's what they would do. Light another match while I look into this niche. Then we will be making tracks for the outside."

Tad was back by Stacy's side a moment later. He motioned that they were to go back. The boys started briskly for the opening. The instant they had crawled out into the outer chamber they realized that all was not as it should be. At first they did not understand what had occurred.

Tad was the first to make the discovery of what had occurred.

"We're caught!" he cried.

"H - ho - how?"

"The tree has closed the opening to the cave. Now we are in a nice pickle."

Stacy was speechless. He held a burning match in his hand until the match burned up to his finger, whereat Chunky dropped the match with an exclamation.

"I - I'll tell you what let's do. Let's dig through the roots. We can do it. Come on."

Tad laid a restraining hand on the fat boy's arm.

"We won't do that just yet. This may have been an accident. Those stones may have slipped off. I am inclined to think that is what has happened. If so, we don't want to leave any clues -"

"I'd rather leave clues than to leave my dead body in here," wailed Chunky.

"Buck up! Don't show a yellow streak, Chunky!" commanded Tad sharply.

"I'm not yellow. But I know enough to know when I've got enough. I know I've got enough of this bandit-chasing business. I ought to have known better than to go out with you. They think I can't keep out of trouble. I can keep out of trouble all right if other folks don't lead me into it. Now see what a fix you've got me into, Tad Butler!"

"It strikes me that I am in the same fix. But we're going to get out of it, Stacy -"

"Yes, but how?"

"I don't know, but I'll find a way."

"Why, we'll starve to death in here. They'll find our bones here a few years from now and they'll wonder - I wish I had something to eat."

"Tighten your belt. Remember, whatever occurs, you are to leave your revolver in its holster. Don't you dare to draw it unless I tell you to. One little slip might be the death of us. For once in your life be prudent."

"I'll be prudent, but I wish I had a sandwich. Have you looked to see if there's anything to eat in this hole?"

"No, I have something of more importance than food to think about at present."

Tad struck a match, taking a long, careful look about the outer chamber of the cave. He saw nothing to encourage him. Rocks everywhere, with here and there a discolored spot where tiny streams had trickled through, perhaps during a heavy rainstorm.

Tad was thinking with all his might, trying to devise some plan by which they might protect themselves in case they were surprised by the return of the bandits, which he did not think would occur before night, even if then. He reasoned that the bandits were far away else the Rangers would not have gone on a long journey in search of them. That meant that the bandits would not be likely to return until matters had quieted down and the Rangers had left the locality.

"I am afraid we are in here for a long stay, old chap,"

Butler said finally.

"Another case of being buried alive, eh?" questioned Stacy. "I told you so. I always am right. But I wasn't when I trusted myself to you. You can get into more trouble, and faster than -"

"At least I don't try to shave the professor with my revolver," retorted Tad sharply. "Hark! What was that?"

"I - I didn't hear anything."

"Sh-h-h!" Tad gripped the arm of his companion. Stacy repressed an "ouch" with some difficulty. The two lads stood listening.

Particles of dirt were rattling from the roots of the fallen tree, sounding like hailstones as they fell to the rocks in the cave. Then a faint ray of light appeared under the bottom of the mass of roots.

"Somebody is coming," whispered Tad. "Stand perfectly still until I tell you to move."

"They can't see us at once. Don't make a sound on your life."

"Wha - what are you going to do?" whispered Stacy, his teeth chattering audibly.

"Duck, if I get half a chance. But I don't think I shall. There it goes!"

The great mass of roots rose clear of the ground, exposing the full height of the opening, and the eyes of the two Pony Rider Boys grew large at what they beheld there in the framed circle of light,

Frank Gee Patchin

CHAPTER XXIII

IN A PERILOUS POSITION

As root mass swung upward, a man with a vicious slap on the animal's thigh, sent a horse bounding in. He followed the horse. Then after him came five other men, crowding in with every appearance of haste. Not a word had been spoken up to this time.

"Now run for your life!" whispered Tad in the ear of his companion. "No, this way. Stoop low. I don't want to get pinned in that other place."

Tad had been using his eyes while glancing about the compartment, and using them to good purpose. He had espied a heap of blankets, either discarded ones or some that had been used for the ponies. He was inclined to the former opinion. He was quite sure that blankets would not be used for the animals at this time of the year. At any rate there was now no time for reflection. It was a time for quick action.

Leading Chunky to the heap, which lay under a projecting ledge of rock some four feet from the floor, Tad forced his companion over behind the pile, then himself crawled in, puffing the blankets over them.

Stacy's teeth were still chattering.

"Stop it!" commanded Tad, giving the fat boy a violent pinch.

This time Chunky did say "ouch!" But before the word was out of his mouth Tad had clapped a blanket over the offending mouth.

"Do you want to be killed?"

"N - n - no."

"Then keep still!"

"Wha - what are they doing?"

"That is what I want to find out if you will lie quiet and not give me any further trouble. They are staking their horses. This must be the stable. The men, as I thought, will go back further. I hope we can hear what they say."

"I don't care what they say. I want to get out of here."

"You never will if you don't muzzle yourself. Now do try to keep quiet while I listen."

Tad raised his head cautiously, but quickly drew it back. What he had seen was the face of the man who had passed himself off as captain of the Rangers when visiting the camp of the Pony Rider Boys a few days before that. This was Willie Jones, the man for whom every Ranger in the state was searching at that moment. And then - Tad shivered in spite of himself when he made the discovery - stepping up to the leader to ask him a question was Dunk Tucker, the fellow whom Tad had captured. Dunk had regained his freedom and had joined his band. His presence here indicated that it was not a good place for the Pony Rider Boys. Tad hoped his own fellows might keep close to their camp. He wondered if the Rangers would be able to trace the bandits to their lair, or if the former even knew the outlaws had returned to that locality again. The words of Tucker answered his question.

"Well, we outrode them, Cap," said Tucker.

"Yes, but if you hadn't made a fool of yourself and tried a pot shot on McKay they wouldn't have known we were anywhere about. That was a fool play on your part, Dunk. Your temper will be the death of you. We'll be lucky if it isn't the death of the whole outfit. I don't want any more of it. If you can't control yourself better, the word will go out that you aren't safe. You know what that means?"

Dunk grinned maliciously.

"I reckon I do. How long we going to stay in here this time?"

"I'll let you know when I am ready to go."

"But ain't you going to clean out that camp?"

"If you mean the boys, I am not. I am looking for bigger game just now. When we get through you can settle your little grudge if you want to. I reckon you'll get your fingers burnt, the same way you did before, if you try it. Those boys are pretty slick."

Tucker's face grew black. No need to tell Tad of what the outlaw was thinking at that moment. He was thinking of the time when the boys had made him a prisoner and how they had been responsible for his having been taken to El Paso and locked up. There was murder in the heart of Dunk Tucker at that moment, as Tad Butler well knew.

The men had lighted candles and stuck them in crevices in the rocks, so that the chamber was fairly well lighted. The horses were white with foam, showing that they had been ridden hard. The watching boy understood. The bandits had been hard pressed by the Rangers.

Jones walked away, leaving Tucker standing there nursing his deadly rage. After a time Dunk followed into the other chamber, where the men fell to discussing their escape in tones plainly audible to the boys hidden under the blankets. From the conversation Tad drew that the men had been on a raid and that they had been forced to throw away much of their plunder because of having been so hard pressed by the pursuing Rangers. Still, three small packs had been unloaded from the ponies in the cave and carried to the inner chamber. The outlaws were not in good humor. Their leader was the only one whose face reflected a smile. Willie could smile even when facing a gun. That smile had upset more than one man's aim and saved Willie's life. Jones fully realized the value of his disconcerting smile.

Tad's reflections were interrupted by the voice of one of the outlaws.

"They're here," said the voice. "I'd like to take a pot at them."

"It'll be your last if you try it," threatened Jones. "This is the only safe retreat we've got. We don't propose to give it away by any, such fool play as shooting at a Ranger from it, much as we'd like to get rid of some of those fellows. They're crowding us pretty close. And right here, I've got a proposition to make. By the way, Gregg, what are they doing?"

"Looking for trails."

The outlaw captain smiled grimly.

"Let 'em look. Precious little trail they'll find, and precious little good it'll do them if they do find it."

"Joe said those stones weren't where he'd left them."

"That's all right. Probably some of those boys have been fooling around here. They're a nosey crowd. But there's no chance that they have discovered anything yet. Give them time and they may. Once we break up the Ranger camp the boys will take French leave mighty quick. It will be too warm for them here. As I was about to say, I have a proposition to make to you. Until things quiet down a little it is my suggestion that we get across the Rio Grande and go into retreat there in our old joint. We've got a lot of valuable stuff here that we can't get out at present and we'll have to leave it here. The Rangers are watching this locality altogether too closely for comfort so far as we are concerned. Withem is nosing around El Paso as you know, lying low for some folks that we know of there. No use to take chances when we don't have to. If you're all agreed we'll just slope to the other side of the river and lie low for a month. What's your idea?"

"I'm agreed, if you'll give me a chance to get even with that gang of boys first," spoke up Tucker.

"You mean that you want to stay here after we've gone?" smiled Captain Willie.

"I reckoned I'd like to until I'd done what I told you."

"Well, I reckon you won't do anything of the sort. When we go out of here, none of us comes back till the whole crowd returns. Is that clear, Dunk?"

The outlaw growled an unintelligible reply.

"The Rangers have drawn off, Captain," called the lookout.

"Which way?"

"Toward the camp."

"They're going to stay there all night," decided the leader. "Well, we'll watch our chance and perhaps we'll be able to get away some time late in the night. Are you all agreed on getting across the river if we can make it?"

The men said they were.

"Then that's settled. Get out the grub. We'll feed up while we've got the chance."

No fire was built. The men munched their food cold. Little was said among them.

And now Tad began to ponder over certain other

phases of his situation. How were these outlaws going to get out? There surely must be some way of opening the way to the outside. Still, the boy did not see how they could move the tree from the inside. If they could do it he could. He decided, however, that it would not be safe to trust to his finding the secret of the opening. Far better would it be to bolt at the first opportunity.

Stacy had kept unusually quiet, though his eyes had grown large when he heard the conversation of the men. At least there was a peep-hole through which the lookout was keeping watch. It occurred to Chunky that he could yell after the men left, and thus attract the attention of his own fellows. Tad had a different idea in mind, though he had not yet fully formulated his plans along this line.

The outlaws having finished their lunch, some rolled up in their blankets and went to sleep undisturbed by the fact that a band of Rangers was encamped within a short quarter of a mile of them.

As for the boys who were in such a tight place, they hardly dared move for fear of frightening the horses and thus exciting the suspicions of the outlaws further down the underground passage. When the boys did change their positions it was done as cautiously as they knew how. One Pony near them evidently scented them, for it grew restless and kept snorting, but that was all.

The hours dragged on wearily. The boys did not know whether it were night or day. Finally the lookout came down to where Jones was pacing steadily back and forth.

"Well?"

"Something going on over there," answered the lookout, jerking his head toward the opening.

"What do you think?"

"I don't know. They're running around out there with torches."

"Where are they?"

"On the other side of the clearing."

"Got their rifles with them?"

"No."

"McKay there?"

"The whole crowd's there."

"They've missed us," whispered Chunky. "They're looking for us."

"Sh - h - h - h," warned Tad softly. Jones pondered for a moment, then he turned to the lookout sharply.

"Wake up the men," he said.

"I reckon something is going to be did," whispered the irrepressible Chunky. Something was.

CHAPTER XXIV

CONCLUSION

The waking of the men was a matter of seconds merely. A touch on the shoulder and the man touched was on his feet as if propelled by springs, hand instinctively going to the revolver dangling from his belt.

Tad, now keenly alive to what was going on, had partially thrown the blankets off, Chunky having done the same.

"Don't stir. I'll tell you when it is time to move," warned Tad.

"Men, I've changed my mind," announced the leader. "Are you ready for a fight?"

"Sure we are if it's Rangers you want us to fight," answered a voice.

"Yes, it's the same old crowd, and a bunch of youngsters thrown in. I don't know what the trouble is, but they're racing around out there with torches -"

"Mebby they've found the trail," suggested one.

"No, I reckon some of the youngsters have strayed away and got lost. All the better for us. The Rangers won't be looking for us."

"They have left their rifles in the camp. They've got their revolvers with them, of course. Take your rifles. Put out all the lights, then while the watch is being kept we'll step out and give them a volley. Be careful to get to one side of the opening so we don't draw their attention too sharply to the opening. That might leave some marks and lead them to investigate when day comes. We'll be a long way from here by that time, but I hope we'll leave a few dead Rangers behind us."

Dunk Tucker was grinning broadly. This was the opportunity for which he had longed.

"Sneak out quietly. Take a good aim. Give them a rattler of a volley. Every man pick his mark. You can't miss. I'll look for McKay. But don't all aim at the same mark or you won't do much damage."

Tad could not repress a shudder. He realized the desperateness of Willie Jones' character fully now. A man who could plan such a cold-blooded crime could have no heart. And the worst of it was that Tad saw no way to prevent the crime.

"How about it up there?"

"They're over in the bush now."

"I want them when they are just outside the bush. If their backs are turned toward us, all the better. We'll give them a hot dose that will give them something to think about," jeered Willie.

"Well, isn't he the cold-blooded fish?" whispered Chunky. "I'd like to take a pot shot at him right where he stands."

"So should I," answered Tad. "But I couldn't do it, bad as he is."

"No, I guess it wouldn't be exactly prudent," returned the fat boy.

"That wasn't what I meant. Prudence hasn't anything to do with it. It would be cold-blooded."

"Ready! Work the lever," commanded the captain as the voice of the lookout called down the one word "Right!"

"Get ready," whispered Tad. "I'm going to bolt. Don't make a sound. We may lose our lives, but I'm going to save the others. If I shoot, drop in your tracks, but be careful not to drop in the opening. Now think as you never thought before!"

"Wha - what are you going to do?" stammered the fat boy.

"Watch me. I can't explain it to you now. There goes the tree."

The operation of the huge bulk was very simple. One of the men procured a long pole from a crevice in the rock. This he thrust down under the roots of the tree, adjusted it and then began working the pole as one would a pump handle. The tree began to rise at once. Tad saw that the outlaw was working a pneumatic jack, on which he figured a piece of timber had been placed so as not to crumble the dirt from the roots when the bulk was raised by the jack. From the outside the bandits no doubt used the same method that the Pony Rider Boys had used to gain an entrance.

"Keep clear of the opening and don't shoot until we're all ready. One volley will be enough, then back and trip the jack. All ready!"

The men began creeping out, Willie Jones in the lead.

"Now!" whispered Tad. "Follow me! Look out for squalls! Things will happen rapidly when they begin."

The boys crept out, following the outlaws as closely as they dared. Once outside the bandits quickly skulked off to one side or the other.

"Get down quick!" whispered Tad.

"Bang, bang, bang!"

Tad Butler fired three shots from his revolver, then threw himself on the ground. Almost with the first shot he heard the voice of the Ranger captain. McKay, ever on the alert, was not caught napping.

"Throw torches away! Down!" he roared.

A thundering volley crashed from the rifles of the outlaws, answered by a rattling fire from the revolvers of the Rangers. Tad heard an outlaw utter an exclamation of pain and knew that one at least of the bad men had been raked by a bullet.

"Back!" came the command from the leader of the

bandits. The word was not spoken loud enough to be heard far away, but every man there heard it, and back they rushed into the cave. A shower of dirt fell over the two Pony Rider Boys, who were by this time crawling on all fours to get away from the tree that they knew would come down with a bump.

It did. The Rangers were still shooting. Tad and Stacy were in a dangerous position. The Rangers were firing right over them. The instant the boys heard the base of the tree fall into place, Tad uttered the owl call.

"Don't shoot, don't shoot!" howled Chunky.

"It's the boys! Stand fast. Lie low!" commanded the Ranger captain. "Something is going on here that we don't know about."

A moment later Tad and Chunky came staggering into the arms of their friends.

"Surround the base of the tree. They're in the cave," cried Tad.

"Wait, wait!" commanded the Ranger.

In the cave the outlaws were beginning to think. Tad's shots had been laid to the carelessness of one of the men. Each one denied that he had fired them.

"That was a signal. Somebody here is a traitor!" cried the leader.

Out there in front of the cave Tad was rapidly whispering to the Ranger captain what had occurred. He told him the bandits were all in the cave and that he believed the only exit was there behind the roots of the big tree.

"Boys, we've got 'em!" cried Billy. "We've got 'em in a trap. Hurrah! Tad, you've saved the lives of some of us. That was as brave a thing as ever a Ranger did and I'll tell you what I think about it after we have smoked those ruffians out."

The smoking-out process was a matter of some time. At the captain's direction, a row of fires was built in front of the cave so that none of the outlaws could escape. On each side of the row of bonfires McKay placed flanking parties who stood with rifles ready to train on the opening should the bandits seek to escape.

All that night and the following day did the Rangers keep silent watch over the cave. The second night fires were built up as before, and part of the force stood watch while the others slept on the ground with rifles for pillows.

It was not until about noon of the third day that any sign of life was observed in the cave. Willie Jones hailed the captain, declaring that he was ready to surrender. Terms were quickly made. The men were to walk out singly, leaving their arms in the cave. There was no need to caution Willie Jones as to what would follow the least sign of treachery. He knew without being told. Grim Rangers were standing on one side so that they should have a clear shooting space in front of them. Billy McKay stood directly facing the opening, as if for the purpose of tempting one of those desperate men in there to take a shot at him. None had the pluck to try it.

Jones was the first one out. He was manacled and searched. One by one the bandits emerged until every man was a prisoner.

That afternoon all were on their way to El Paso. It would be many years before they would again terrorize the Rio Grande border if at all, for there were many charges against them. Among the charges preferred against the bandits was that of aiding the Germans by stirring up trouble on the border. Not a man confessed, but while the government was unable to prove this particular charge, it was positive that in the arrest of this desperate gang a nest of dangerous traitors had been broken up.

The entire credit for the capture was given to the two Pony Rider Boys, Tad Butler and Stacy Brown. The Pony Rider Boys party accompanied the Rangers to El Paso, whence, later on, they continued their journey down the Rio Grande. The boys were praised by every one for their bravery, and especially were Tad and Stacy, who had so bravely risked their own lives to save the lives of their young companions and the Rangers.

A big reward was earned by the Rangers, but at Captain McKay's suggestion, a thousand dollars was turned over to Professor Zepplin to be divided between Tad and Chunky later on. The professor's protests availed him nothing. McKay said the professor might throw the money in the gutter if he didn't want it, so the professor sent the thousand dollars to the father of Walter Perkins. That gentleman deposited it to the credit of the two plucky young lads, though it was some time ere they knew the existence of this special fund, all their own.

It was the last night in camp before ending their wonderful outing, and every one was solemn-eyed and thoughtful. Their playspell was at an end and they were sad. Tad and Ned were speaking of the war, each confiding his desire to the other, to get into the fight, and expressing his intention of doing so soon.

"Professor," called Tad. "We know of course how you feel on the subject, but this is a good time for us all to make our confessions, on this the last night of our season's outing, and know where we stand on the war."

"We are all patriots here," interjected Walter Perkins.

"All but one and he's a German," spoke up Stacy Brown. "I refer to that noble man, Professor Zepplin, first cousin to the airship known as a Zeppelin -"

Professor Zepplin's whiskers fairly bristled.

"Young man, that will do!" he thundered. "I am an American citizen, and you have no right to question my loy -"

"There, there, Professor, don't you know Chunky by this time? All he wished was to draw your fire and stir you up, which I reckon he's done," soothed Tad laughingly.

Stacy chuckled under his breath, at the same time keeping a weather eye out for any hostile move that Professor Zepplin might make, for the professor plainly was excited.

"That is all very well, young men," returned the professor. "I know that you know what my

Americanism is. I have no need to tell you that, but, as Tad says, this is a good time for us all to declare our loyalty, and we should reiterate it every day of our lives."

"That's the talk," cried Ned Rector.

"As you boys know, I was born in Germany. I attended a German military school and, to cut the story short, I became a German officer. I fought in many battles -"

"At the battle of the Nile he was fitting all the while," murmured the fat boy under his breath. Tad rebuked Stacy with a look.

"One day, after I had served my time, I emigrated to America. It was not until then that I realized that I had been wrong, that I had been upholding an unworthy cause. That was years ago. Soon I had absorbed the spirit of American liberty and became at one with its ideals. I became a citizen. Of course I looked back on my army experience with a certain amount of pride. No one who has fought and bled can help doing that - up to a certain point."

"I can well understand that," murmured Tad. "I think I know how you felt."

"When Germany made war on little Belgium and France my pride of service turned to regret. I was sorry deep down in my heart that I had served the Fatherland, but I rejoiced that I was then an American, a loyal American. It was when - when the despicable Huns sank the Lusitania, the most dastardly crime in the world's history, that my soul was suddenly filled with loathing. I offered my services to the country of my adoption, believing that they would go to war at once, but I was too old, and then America was not yet prepared for the great conflict. Since we went to war I have again offered my services. I can still fight, young men."

"I should say you can," interjected Tad.

"My name, at this time, is an unfortunate one," continued the professor. "It is not the name, but the heart that counts, and my heart is in and for America, and my life and all that I have or ever shall have is hers for the asking."

The Pony Rider Boys with one accord sprang to their feet and, tossing their hats in the air, uttered a wild cowboy yell. Professor Zepplin held up a hand.

"Wait!" he commanded. "There is something yet to be done and now is the time to do it." Thrusting a hand into a pocket he drew forth a leather case and opened it with unsteady fingers. From the case he drew a small object wrapped in tissue paper.

"The Iron Cross," murmured the boys.

"Yes, it is the Iron Cross," agreed the professor. "Time was when this was my most priceless possession. Now I loathe it. Its possession has troubled me greatly of late and it has been my intention to rid myself of the hateful thing. Boys, what shall be done with it?"

"That is for you to say, Professor," answered Tad in a low voice.

"Get an axe," advised Chunky.

"Yes, yes, the axe," agreed the professor.

Tad handed the tool to the professor. The latter placed the once prized decoration on a stone and with one blow from the axe smashed the cross. Blow after blow he rained on the medal until it lay scattered in pieces. These the professor gathered up and hurled far from him.

"That is what I think of Germany, monarchial Germany, the assassin of innocent women and children."

"Boys, 'The Star-spangled Banner,'" cried Tad after a moment of impressive silence.

The youthful voices of the Pony Rider Boys rose in the National anthem, the deep bass voice of Professor Zepplin booming out above all the rest.

When next we meet our boys we shall find them in utterly different surroundings. In the next volume of the present series our readers will find an extremely fascinating tale. It is published under the title, *The Pony Rider Boys On The Blue Ridge; Or, A Lucky Find in the Carolina Mountains.*

Choose from Thousands of 1stWorldLibrary Classics By

Adolphus WilliamWard
Aesop
Agatha Christie
Alexander Aaronsohn
Alexander Kielland
Alexandre Dumas
Alfred Gatty
Alfred Ollivant
Alice Duer Miller
Alice Turner Curtis
Alice Dunbar
Ambrose Bierce
Amelia E. Barr
Andrew Lang
Andrew McFarland Davis
Anna Sewell
Annie Besant
Annie Hamilton Donnell
Annie Payson Call
Anton Chekhov
Arnold Bennett
Arthur Conan Doyle
Arthur Ransome
Atticus
B. M. Bower
Basil King
Bayard Taylor
Ben Macomber
Booth Tarkington
Bram Stoker
C. Collodi
C. E. Orr
C. M. Ingleby
Carolyn Wells
Catherine Parr Traill
Charles A. Eastman
Charles Dickens
Charles Dudley Warner
Charles Farrar Browne
Charles Ives
Charles Kingsley
Charles Lathrop Pack
Charles Whibley
Charles Willing Beale
Charlotte M. Braeme
Charlotte M.Yonge
Clair W. Hayes
Clarence Day Jr.
Clarence E. Mulford

Clemence Housman
Confucius
Cornelis DeWitt Wilcox
Cyril Burleigh
D. H. Lawrence
Daniel Defoe
David Garnett
Don Carlos Janes
Donald Keyhole
Dorothy Kilner
Dougan Clark
E. Nesbit
E.P.Roe
E. Phillips Oppenheim
Edgar Allan Poe
Edgar Rice Burroughs
Edith Wharton
Edward J. O'Biren
John Cournos
Edwin L. Arnold
Eleanor Atkins
Elizabeth Cleghorn
Gaskell
Elizabeth Von Arnim
Ellem Key
Emily Dickinson
Erasmus W. Jones
Ernie Howard Pie
Ethel Turner
Ethel Watts Mumford
Eugenie Foa
Eugene Wood
Evelyn Everett-Green
Everard Cotes
F. J. Cross
Federick Austin Ogg
Ferdinand Ossendowski
Francis Bacon
Francis Darwin
Frances Hodgson Burnett
Frank Gee Patchin
Frank Harris
Frank Jewett Mather
Frank L. Packard
Frederick Trevor Hill
Frederick Winslow Taylor
Friedrich Kerst
Friedrich Nietzsche
Fyodor Dostoyevsky

Gabrielle E. Jackson
Garrett P. Serviss
Gaston Leroux
George Ade
Geroge Bernard Shaw
George Ebers
George Eliot
George MacDonald
George Orwell
George Tucker
George W. Cable
George Wharton James
Gertrude Atherton
Grace E. King
Grant Allen
Guillermo A. Sherwell
Gulielma Zollinger
Gustav Flaubert
H. A. Cody
H. B. Irving
H. G. Wells
H. H. Munro
H. Irving Hancock
H. Rider Haggard
H. W. C. Davis
Hamilton Wright Mabie
Hans Christian Andersen
Harold Avery
Harold McGrath
Harriet Beecher Stowe
Harry Houidini
Helent Hunt Jackson
Helen Nicolay
Hendy David Thoreau
Henrik Ibsen
Henry Adams
Henry Ford
Henry Frost
Henry James
Henry Jones Ford
Henry Seton Merriman
Henry Wadsworth
Longfellow
Henry W Longfellow
Herbert A. Giles
Herbert N. Casson
Herman Hesse
Homer
Honore De Balzac

Horace Walpole
Horatio Alger, Jr.
Howard Pyle
Howard R. Garis
Hugh Lofting
Hugh Walpole
Humphry Ward
Ian Maclaren
Israel Abrahams
J.G.Austin
J. Henri Fabre
J. M. Barrie
J. Macdonald Oxley
J. S. Knowles
J. Storer Clouston
Jack London
Jacob Abbott
James Allen
James Lane Allen
James Andrews
James Baldwin
James DeMille
James Joyce
James Oliver Curwood
James Oppenheim
James Otis
Jane Austen
Jens Peter Jacobsen
Jerome K. Jerome
John Burroughs
John F. Kennedy
John Gay
John Glasworthy
John Habberton
John Joy Bell
John Milton
John Philip Sousa
Jonathan Swift
Joseph Carey
Joseph Conrad
Joseph Jacobs
Julian Hawthrone
Julies Vernes
Justin Huntly McCarthy
Kakuzo Okakura
Kenneth Grahame
Kate Langley Bosher
L. A. Abbot
L. T. Meade
L. Frank Baum
Laura Lee Hope

Laurence Housman
Leo Tolstoy
Leonid Andreyev
Lewis Carroll
Lilian Bell
Lloyd Osbourne
Louis Tracy
Louisa May Alcott
Lucy Fitch Perkins
Lucy Maud Montgomery
Lydia Miller Middleton
Lyndon Orr
M. H. Adams
Margaret E. Sangster
Margaret Vandercook
Maria Edgeworth
Maria Thompson Daviess
Mariano Azuela
Marion Polk Angellotti
Mark Overton
Mark Twain
Mary Austin
Mary Cole
Mary Rowlandson
Mary Wollstonecraft Shelley
Max Beerbohm
Myra Kelly
Nathaniel Hawthrone
O. F. Walton
Oscar Wilde
Owen Johnson
P.G.Wodehouse
Paul and Mable Thorn
Paul G. Tomlinson
Paul Severing
Peter B. Kyne
Plato
R. Derby Holmes
R. L. Stevenson
Rabindranath Tagore
Rahul Alvares
Ralph Waldo Emmerson
Rene Descartes
Rex E. Beach
Richard Harding Davis
Richard Jefferies
Robert Barr
Robert Frost
Robert Gordon Anderson
Robert L. Drake

Robert Lansing
Robert Michael Ballantyne
Robert W. Chambers
Rosa Nouchette Carey
Ross Kay
Rudyard Kipling
Samuel B. Allison
Samuel Hopkins Adams
Sarah Bernhardt
Selma Lagerlof
Sherwood Anderson
Sigmund Freud
Standish O'Grady
Stanley Weyman
Stella Benson
Stephen Crane
Stewart Edward White
Stijn Streuvels
Swami Abhedananda
Swami Parmananda
T. S. Ackland
The Princess Der Ling
Thomas A. Janvier
Thomas A Kempis
Thomas Anderton
Thomas Bailey Aldrich
Thomas Bulfinch
Thomas De Quincey
Thomas H. Huxley
Thomas Hardy
Thomas More
Thornton W. Burgess
U. S. Grant
Valentine Williams
Victor Appleton
Virginia Woolf
Walter Scott
Washington Irving
Wilbur Lawton
Wilkie Collins
Willa Cather
Willard F. Baker
William Makepeace Thackeray
William W. Walter
Winston Churchill
Yei Theodora Ozaki
Young E. Allison
Zane Grey

www.ingramcontent.com/pod-product-compliance
Lightning Source LLC
Chambersburg PA
CBHW050033180626
46810CB00002B/701